D1557084

COME ON IN,

I'LL TELL YOU A STORY

ALSO BY PETER HORNBOSTEL

The Ambassador to Brazil

COME ON IN,

I'LL TELL YOU A STORY

Peter Hornbostel

Book design by Mirko Pohl

ISBN – 9798567105252

1. World War II – Fiction. 2. Jungles - Amazon River Region –
Fiction. 3. Brazil - Rio de Janeiro – Fiction. 4. Virginia - Shenandoah
Valley – Fiction.

For Monika, Susan and Lise

Come on in,

I'll Tell You a Story

Contents

THEATRE

I was going to tell you a little about Brazil, like the Garota de Ipanema and the Carnival parade and the girls on the beach and *futebol*. And I still will...just not yet. You'll have to wait a little.

That's because the publisher has asked me first to tell you a little more about myself. If you want to be published, you don't ignore your publisher's request.

And so I'm going to leave Brazil aside for a few moments and introduce myself instead. My name is Peter Hornbostel, although that's not what my birth certificate says. It says Peter Rosenbaum. I can show it to you, if you like. I've spent my professional life as an international lawyer, but that's not what I really would like to be. I'm also a writer, a storyteller, a director, and an actor. That's what I really wanted to be.

My story really begins in Berlin three years before I was born. It was 1933. My mother, Anni Caro, was married to the famous German Jewish psychologist Max Rosenbaum, although her affair with my father had already begun. Rosenbaum, the father of the Gestalt theory of psychology, was some 53 years old at the time. My mother was 32. There were three children, my brother Val, who was then nine, my brother Mike, who was seven, and Lise, who was six.

Although Hitler was not yet *Reichskanzler*, the handwriting was on the wall, and one of Rosenbaum's colleagues at the University of Berlin suggested that Professor Rosenbaum listen to the Fuhrer on the radio, next time he spoke. He did, together with my mother. When the speech was over, he walked over, switched off the radio, and said to my mother "*wir mussen gehen*" ("we must go").

"Yes," she said. "But when?"

"Tomorrow morning," he said. And in fact, they did.

They went first to Prague, which was still free in 1933, where the professor had a second house. There they organized their things, and booked passage on the Q.E. to New York, where Max had a job waiting for him at the New School. I wouldn't have been part of all this, in fact I would not be a part of this world at all, if my mother's lover, Johannes von Hornbostel, who later changed his name to John, a young research physicist, had not followed close behind.

There was no job awaiting him in New York. He lived

2

alone in a fourth story walk-up room in the Bronx, working when he could for a doctor whom he had known on the "other side", and who was developing certain improvements on the x-ray machine. Anni would visit him once a week, on Saturday afternoon, until everything changed in 1941.

Professor Rosenbaum's comfortable house in New Rochelle soon became a center of expatriates, mostly of Jewish intellectual activity. The language of the house was German (although Rosa, the cheerful black cook, her husband Albert, and Lillian, who did the laundry, spoke only English). Paul Tillich was a frequent visitor, as was Albert Einstein, who usually came for Sunday dinner and stayed to participate in the weekly string quartet.

Max on the cello, Einstein on first violin, my mother as second violin, and someone I can't remember on viola. Years later I asked my mother how well Einstein played. "Albert," she said. "Albert played very nicely. He just couldn't count."

My mother would later tell me that Einstein used to bounce me on his knee when I was a baby. Maybe that was the reason, she said, that I seem to have my brains in my bottom. "Osmosis," she said.

I came along in 1936. I was conceived, according to my mother, on an overnight trip on a small steamer that plied the Atlantic coast between New York and New Haven. My father viewed the pregnancy as a total disaster that was certain to result in a major scandal. He proposed that my mother and he gather

3

together their love letters in a suitcase, and that they then leap off the George Washington bridge into the Hudson, the suitcase tied to their wrists. My mother laughed at him, and the idea ended there. I still have that suitcase, but I have never read the letters.

Anni went to Max and told him she was pregnant. He knew, of course, that the child was not his. He and Anni had not slept together since before they had arrived in New York. But Max felt that everyone would be better off, especially the children, if Max were assumed to be the father of the child. He and Anni made a solemn agreement that Val, Mike and Lise would not be told.

My mother drove herself, on October 29, 1936, to the Women's Hospital in Manhattan. Max did not know how to drive, and my father, who came along in the back seat, was too nervous. She parked in front of the hospital on West 110th Street and rushed in, fearing her water could break at any moment. When she reemerged four days later, with me on her arm and my birth certificate in her pocket, the Buick was still there, but the seats had been stolen.

I don't know how we got back to New Rochelle, someone must have come to fetch us, but I do know that replacement seats were considered too expensive. Max bought a set of used dining room chairs and had them bolted into the car. To this day, I worry about seats. Are there enough? Are there too many? Will they be empty? You may doubt that these worries have anything to do with that seat crisis when I was four days old. I don't remember that crisis. But who knows?

The next five years may have been some of the best years of my life. There is not much that I remember, but a few pictures come floating up into my consciousness, still there, close to a century later. I'll try to show them to you.

First, there was the house, a big old Victorian at 12, The Circle, in New Rochelle, with a large yard in the back. "The Circle" was a circular park that seemed to me at the time gigantic, across the road from our house, which seemed to me gigantic as well. I went back to try and find the house just after last Christmas. It was still there, painted a dull brown, and looking a little down at the heels. It had shrunk, of course, and the big tree where my swing had been was gone. But the house is still there. And The Circle is still gigantic. The biggest change is the ten lane freeway, which hums night and day just behind the houses on the opposite side of The Circle. Life itself goes coursing by on the freeway, and the house remains behind.

I don't remember much about the inside of the house, but I know there was an upright piano in the back hall, and on Sunday nights Max, whose name was "Papsen" to us kids, would get out the Gilbert and Sullivan song book, it was green and a little ragged and would play the piano while Val, Mike and Lise sang along. I was there too, and I sat on someone's lap, or on the floor along the wall. I don't remember if I sang too, probably not, but I still know most of the songs in the H.M.S. Pinafore. I still have that book. There are a few of Max's notations in it, but I can't make them out.

After the singing someone would take me up to bed. I slept in my mother's room, where she had a single bed. Max's room, where he slept, studied, and wrote his learned books and articles was across the hall. My bed was in the corner by the door. The light from the hall came in from behind my head and shone on the wall in front, which made a perfect stage for the shadow figures of geese and rabbits and dogs and cats, and even squirrels which Papsen made with his hands from the doorway until I fell asleep. Most nights Lise or Mike would be there as well, out in the hall, watching the show. It was theater, brought down to our size.

Mike and Lise were the best fun of all. Up on the third floor, in the room next to where Rosa, the cook, slept, were two old twin beds. Sometimes Mike, sometimes Lise would take me there, and bounce, and bounce, and bounce, higher and higher, until poor Max, whose room was just underneath, would trudge up the stairs and take us all out into the back garden, and ask Rosa to bring us some lemonade and cookies. And if it was hot, he would get out the hose, and I would take off my clothes, and he would hose me down while I shrieked. There are some pictures of me, with clothes and without, clowning for the camera out in the garden, with an audience consisting of Papsen, my mother, Mike, Lise, sometimes Val. I loved it.

And then there were those wonderful times with Lise. There were these three games she had made up, and which she played with me almost every day. One was called the Enormouse - mouse (me). I can't quite remember the game, but it involved her putting me way up high on a branch, or a bench, or a low roof. She was always there to catch me if I should fall, but I never did.

Then there was "Stiff as a Board". I would stand, make myself "stiff as a board", close my eyes, and then fall backwards on my heels, until Lise caught me, and pushed me back to vertical. Each time she let me fall a little further, until it seemed like I had to hit the ground. But I never did. She was always there. Sometimes Mike would catch me from the front and Lise from the back. I rocked back and forth, farther and farther, stiff as a board, eyes clenched shut. They never let me fall.

And then there was the "Witch". She was a good witch, though she had a terrible cackle. Lise would take me to some place in the garden, tell me to close my eyes, and spin me around a few times. And in a few seconds, the witch would appear to take me on an adventure, crossing a bridge 1,000 feet over a chasm (the garden bench), or poking around a haunted castle (the tool shed), or trying to cross a crowded speedway (the quiet road out front). It was a fine game, so long as you kept your eyes clenched shut. I never opened them. Never.

There was theater in much of this - Max's shadow play, the Gilbert and Sullivan songs, Lise's witch - but that wasn't all. The whole thing was theater, written, produced and directed by Max, with me in the starring role. In Max's play, I was Max's child, he and Anni were happy together, my brothers and sister were just that, not half brothers and sister. Of course, the play was not intended exclusively for my benefit. Lise, Mike and Val had

7

equal places in Papsen's heart. He was father not only of the four of us, but of the Gestalt theory of psychology, as well. He knew that changes in perception of the whole, could change reality itself. And that is what he did, until the whole carefully constructed image came crashing down in 1941, like the end of a play.

Although Papsen was my father, as far as I knew, my mother started telling me in 1940, that I had two fathers. The other was a grey, thin, distant man with one bad eye, which looked off to the left while his good eye looked straight ahead. He appeared occasionally at 12 The Circle in a grey Ford, only long enough to pick up my mother and drive away. He did not talk or look at me, whether with the good eye or the bad one. He was, of course, John Hornbostel, my biological father, and the central figure in my mother's romantic play.

I don't know what caused my mother to conclude, sometime in 1941, that it was time to leave Max and finally marry John Hornbostel. Hornbostel had no interest in children, including his own child, and wanted only to finally have Anni to himself. My mother wouldn't buy this, however. She loved me and felt that I was too young to be left in New Rochelle. Moreover I was, as she was often to say later on, her only "love child". She called Val, Mike and Lise together and explained to them that I was actually Hornbostel's child and that I would be leaving New Rochelle with her.

Anni went by herself to Reno, Nevada and when she

returned eight weeks later with divorce papers in hand, she moved, with my father, into two rented rooms in a big white house in Glen Ridge, New Jersey. I went with her as planned. Val, Mike, Lise, and of course Max remained behind in New Rochelle. My friend, Rosa, the cook, remained as well.

In Glen Ridge life was not the same. It was clear that my father did not want me there, and my siblings and Max, my loving audience, were nowhere to be seen. Max's play, and my leading role in it, had come to an end. There was no part for me in John Hornbostel's play.

Though I tried, for the next 24 years until his death in 1969 to change that, I never succeeded.

One afternoon in 1942, my mother backed the grey Ford rapidly down the driveway of the Glen Ridge house, and stopped where I was playing with some stones near the sidewalk. "Papsen died," she said. "Mrs. Schulte is coming to give you dinner and put you to bed. I'll be back soon. Come give me a kiss." I kissed her and then she was gone. Perhaps she believed that since Papsen was not my biological father, his death should not matter to me. In a way she was right. I had lost him already.

It is not accidental, of course, that we so often follow roughly in the footsteps of our parents, or older siblings, perhaps with a few changes thrown in, just to establish our independence. Mike and Lise both became psychology professors, they write books and scholarly articles. I became a lawyer, following Val's footsteps. But perhaps what I have wanted all along was to

9

recapture the theater that Max, my sister and brothers created during my first five years.

It was the most important theater of my life.

BOLERO

João Custodio dos Santos and Teresinha moved on the floor with the grace and elegance of dancers who had danced together for decades. In fact, they had. You couldn't say the music was graceful. Just loud. They call it the "bolero" in the interior of Brazil, or sometimes just the "rhythm." It has nothing at all to do with a bolero like they dance in Spain. But one night about 60 years ago, a handsome young Mexican gold miner had swept into Ouro Preto and taken the town, or better said, the young women in the town, by storm. The Saturday night dance on the second floor of the *sobrado* on Rua São José was just getting started when the young man strode into the place as the band was playing the first *chorinho* of the night.

"Ah, the bolero," the young man shouted above the music, as he took Maria Aparecida into his arms and began to dance. Three months later Maria Aparecida was pregnant, and they ran the young Spaniard out of town. But the name "bolero" stuck…

João dos Santos was about a meter sixty, that's roughly five foot two in your system, my friend, and Teresinha measured five foot ten in her stocking feet. Had her parents only known, they would have baptized her Teresa, not Teresinha, but at that age you could hardly know, could you? Anyway, by the time she was 19, she was tall, slender as a willow, and unable to put one foot in front of the other without tripping over her own toes.

"Joaquim," said Teresa's mother to her husband one Saturday night some 25 years ago, "perhaps we should take Teresinha with us to the bolero tonight." Sr. Joaquim looked at Dona Esmerelda, his wife, as if she had taken complete leave of her senses, and went back to reading his paper.

"I'm serious, Joaquim. She is so lovely, but so clumsy on her feet. Look what the rhythm did for us when we were courting. Maybe some nice young man will teach her to dance, and perhaps they might even…" her voice trailed away.

"Ok, tá bom," said Sr. Joaquim.

Over the years he had learned that it was easier to simply go along with his wife's crazy ideas than to argue with them. And so, that night 25 years ago, Teresinha danced her first bolero.

I guess you might say danced. Stumbled would be less charitable, but more accurate. As soon as the family entered the hall and sat down at the table which had been theirs every Saturday night for 43 years, a young man came over to the table. He was a little short, perhaps, but Dona Esmerelda was delighted. She shot Sr. Joaquim a victorious glance.

"Would the senhorita care to dance?" João dos Santos asked Teresinha.

Teresinha shook her head a vigorous "no," but her mother quickly answered.

"Oh, she'd be delighted." And so Teresinha, obediently stood up and walked out onto the floor with the young man.

Those good people who were at the dance that night and who are still alive talk about it as a catastrophe. At least that's how they remember it. Dr. Alonso, now 81 years old but still dancing, swears that she fell down twice while going backwards across the floor. José Zacharias, who actually dances with his own wife, remembers Teresinha in tears. But as the evening wore on and they stayed on the dance floor, with much prodding from Dona Esmerelda, things actually began to improve, and if you were generous of spirit, you might even have said that when Teresinha went home with her parents at midnight, she had actually been dancing.

João dos Santos went home walking on air, but also worried. He worked at the São Francisco church, the most beautiful church in the town. Years ago, Dom Manoel had hired him to sweep the church early Sunday mornings before mass.

He had done such a good job that the priest had hired him full time to clean up the church when it was needed, do a little painting, take care of the garden, and, from time to time, go out to buy him a bottle of good rum which, he told João, was needed for religious purposes.

One Sunday morning after mass, the priest had called him aside.

"João," he said, "I have another job for you. I want you to begin dusting the saints before mass on Sundays."

João's breath dropped out of his lungs, tears came to his eyes. The wooden saints in the niches on either side of the nave were from the 18th century or even before. They were the treasures of the town.

"You have careful and caring hands, João," the priest continued. "I can trust you with our saints. And something else, João. If you are willing, I believe we should change your name from João dos Santos to João Custodio dos Santos, John Custodian of the Saints."

It was, as you can imagine, my friends, the happiest moment of his life.

But now, as he walked home through the empty streets of the town, he was worried. Was it alright for a custodian of saints to dance with such a lovely girl, even to teach her to dance? He was sure she was a virgin just like the beautiful Virgin Mary in the second niche to the right. Imagine, if he were teaching the Virgin Mary to dance! The very idea was sacrilegious! That night, João Custodio could not sleep. At times Teresinha moved gracefully through his mind, at times it was the Virgin Mary, at times it was both. If truth be told, he was a little scared of women, especially beautiful ones.

It's not that he didn't like women, it's just that he didn't understand them, just like the rest of us. On Sundays, he usually walked up the hill at 6:00 to prepare for early mass. But this particular morning, as soon as the bells struck 4:00, he put on his shoes and walked up the cobblestones to the back door of the church. He unlocked the door, walked inside, and lit a candle. Then he walked down the right aisle and stopped in front of the Virgin Mary. He left the candle there, and by the light of the street lamp outside, walked back to the janitor's closet, took out his stepladder, and carried it back to the saint. Then he climbed the ladder, took the Virgin Mary ever so carefully in his arms and brought her down the ladder. Then, very slowly, very carefully, he began to dance. I do not know how long he danced, but when the bolero in his mind ended, he held the saint very close to his head and whispered,

"Virgin Mary, Mother of God, what should I do?"

"Dance," said the saint very gently into his ear. "Dance."

And so, every Saturday night for the last 25 years he and Teresinha had danced together at the bolero on the second floor of number 132 on Rua São José.

Physically, they didn't fit together very well, one about five feet tall and the other almost six, but they danced so well together that no one noticed. By now, both of their parents had passed to their heavenly reward. So had Dom Manoel. There was a new priest now, Dom Ricardo, a modern priest who even came to the bolero now and then, although he didn't dance.

One afternoon as they were both working in the garden, he had asked João Custodio how old he was. "52," João Custodio said.

"And you never married," the priest asked.

"No."

"Why not?"

João Custodio thought a long time.

"Father," he said, "how can the custodian of the Virgin Mary, marry someone else?"

The priest laughed. "Don't be silly," he said. He pointed to his collar. "I can't marry," he said. "But you can. And don't you worry about the Virgin Mary. Her real custodian is in heaven. He won't be angry if you take a wife."

João Custodio thought about this for several weeks. Every Saturday night, Teresinha and he continued to dance at the bolero. The slightest pressure on her left hand would send her gliding backward into the space another dancer had just relinquished, the smallest movement of his index finger on her back would send her into a graceful spin back to him.

João Custodio was holding in his arms the slimmest, most

graceful woman in the hall. And they had never been out together. His nose was only slightly above her chest and her perfume, the same she had used at the bolero every Saturday night for the last 25 years, wafted over him.

But his mind was on what the priest had said.

And now Dom Ricardo was sitting at the side of the dance floor, conversing with José Alberto, the town barber, and sipping a lime *caipirinha.* He smiled at João Custodio and winked.

"Well," he thought, "it's now or never."

He gracefully moved Teresinha closer to him, so that her left ear was close to his mouth.

"Would you like to have dinner with me on Monday?" he said.

For the first time in almost 25 years, Teresinha's right foot stepped too close to his left foot, his foot bumped her middle toe, and for a moment, they stumbled out of beat.

"No," she said, and spun out to her left, although he hadn't signaled a spin.

"Thank God," he said. "Me neither."

She spun her body back close to his, their feet back in perfect harmony with the rhythm.

"But we can dance," she said.

ROBERTO'S NOSE

It was pure luck that I was in São Paulo just one day after Roberto died. He had been a very wealthy man, the owner of six large cattle ranches in the interior of Brazil, a major gas distribution facility in the state of São Paulo, several petrochemical plants in the Northeast of Brazil and several other factories scattered around the country. I had been his attorney for many years, negotiating the international financing and technology licenses for his projects. He had treated me more like a son than his attorney, inviting me to his ranches on weekends, as well as dinners at his São Paulo home.

I had a number of clients in Brazil, many of them introduced to me by Roberto. I traveled to South America to see them every few months. My first stop was always Roberto's office in São Paulo. I was a little worried this trip. He was 75 years old and I had heard that he was not well. For the first time, Jorge the operator of Roberto's private office elevator, wasn't there, so I took myself up to the 7th floor. Teresinha, Roberto's secretary was sitting at her desk outside his office. Her eyes were red. She looked as if she had been crying.

"He's gone," she said.

"When?"

"Yesterday. You are very lucky."

I knew just what she meant. The Brazilians don't keep the bodies of their dead around for more than 24 or at the most 48 hours. After that, they are either cremated or buried before they can start to decompose in the heat.

"You can still see him at the Einstein, but you better go right away," Teresinha said.

The Einstein is the best and wealthiest hospital in Brazil. It sits atop one of the hills near the center of São Paulo. Its lowest floor contains a large stone crypt dug into the hill, which is available for viewing the body of a deceased who might die in the hospital and whose family can afford the daily rental of the crypt. There is an elevator that connects the crypt and the hospital rooms above. The elevator ride costs extra.

"I'll have a driver take you over," Teresinha said. "He'll take you straight to the crypt."

The hospital has a long driveway which curves up the hill before it forks and continues to two portals, one to the hospital itself and the other to the crypt. Along the driveway up to the crypt, some 20 or 30 black limousines were parked, Mercedes, Rolls Royces, Cadillacs, and other imports, their chauffeurs leaning against their cars, smoking cigarettes. Against the stone wall along the uphill side of the drive were several large white floral displays, some two meters high or more. There wasn't enough space for the car to get through so I got out and walked up to the ornate wooden door marked "Entrada".

Inside was a small room where Roberto's family sat waiting to greet the mourners who came to pay their respects. Roberto's two widows from his first and second marriages, Ana Maria Tereza and Dona Lidia, were there of course. So too were his two beautiful daughters Elena Maria and Eliana. They welcomed me like family. Pedro and Jorge, their husbands, were out in the adjoining reception hall mingling with the other guests. "Go find them," Maria Tereza said. "They'll be delighted to see you."

There were at least one hundred people, mostly men, in the huge windowless reception hall, chatting, drinking Scotch whiskey and smoking cigars or cigarettes. The presidents of several of my clients were there including Paulo Villares, Max Feffer the owner of Suzano, Aloisio Farias, the owner of Banco Real and his son in law, Luis Enrique, Heinrich Schultz the president of Volkswagen do Brasil and the president of Vale do Rio Doce, the largest mining company in South America. Several directors of Petrobras, the national oil monopoly, were there, as well as a number of important political figures from the state government, and the mayor of the city of São Paulo.

"You made it," said Pedro as he gave me a big Brazilian abraço. I was worried you might not."

Another abraço, this one from Jorge.

"Have you seen him," he asked.

"Not yet," I said.

"Even the Governor was here earlier," Jorge said. "The President of the Republic is in São Paulo on a state visit. He might come. But I can tell you one thing, Senhor Roberto would care more about you being here than about the President."

"Why don't you go in there now," Pedro asked. "I haven't seen anyone go into the crypt for quite a while. You might even have him all to yourself."

I looked around. "Where is it?" I asked.

Jorge pointed at what looked like a gigantic hole in one of the walls. "The crypt is in there," he said. "There is a sort of tunnel. Just walk down it. You'll know when you get there."

"Okay," I said. After all, that is what I was there for.

Just like Jorge had said, the hole emptied into what looked like a long tunnel that had been carved through the rock. Along the sides were still more floral displays with ribbons which read "Roberto Querido Amigão", or "Roberto no Céu", "Roberto Amado Heroi", or other similar phrases. After about two hundred feet of tunnel it opened into the crypt, a large round cave that had been carved in the stone.

There was no light other than one single electric lamp that

hung down from the ceiling, shining on Roberto in his elegant walnut coffin. His face was more somber than I had ever seen it in life. The funeral director who had made him up obviously had not known him.

There was something else that was wrong. Roberto's corpse had been dressed up in a white shirt and a green and yellow striped tie. To be sure, green and yellow were the colors of the Brazilian flag, but Roberto had never worn a necktie in his life. At least not as long as I had known him. If he were alive he surely would have torn it off. I was tempted to tear it off for him now. But I didn't.

There was a more serious problem though: something was wrong with his nose. The size was right but there was definitely something wrong. Was it the color? Did it look too waxy? I couldn't tell just what was wrong, but something wasn't right. I looked again. Then I reached down and gently touched the right side of Roberto's nose. It fell over to the left.

Just then I heard someone starting to walk down the tunnel toward the crypt, speaking with someone in Portuguese. Quickly I picked up Roberto's nose with my left index finger and thumb and set the nose upright as it belonged. It felt just a little bit waxy. The nose fell over again, this time to the right.

I could hear the conversation of the people walking slowly down the tunnel toward the crypt. Quickly I reached for the nose and tried again. This time I used the index fingers of both hands, one on each side of the nose to hold it straight up. It stayed there after I took my fingers away for about three seconds. But it collapsed again!

The conversation of the people walking down the tunnel toward the crypt was getting louder now, although I could hear nothing but the panicked beating of my own heart. I reached down and picked up the nose by its tip and shoved it hard into Roberto's face where it belonged. I heard a sort of slurping sound and the nose stood up straight for about three seconds once again. But when I took my hand away the nose fell over again, this time to the left.

The couple coming down the tunnel were almost to the crypt by now. I could hear their footsteps not so far away. I leaned over Roberto's head and whispered, "Roberto, for the love of God, help me out." As I pulled my head away, I thought I heard a word that seemed to be coming from Roberto's head,

"Puxa," it said. I couldn't quite make it out.

"What?" I said, "Say it again."

Very softly, I heard the voice again.

"Puxa," it said. It sounded like "push" in English but I had already tried that. Then I realized that Roberto's spirit would be speaking Portuguese, not English. "Puxa" in Portuguese means "pull" not "push". I reached down and picked up the nose again by its tip, and I pulled hard upward toward the light. I heard a soft click. Slowly, barely breathing, I took my fingers away just to make sure. The nose continued standing where it was. I gave it a soft nudge. It didn't move.

I stepped back from the casket and whispered, "Thank you Roberto," just as the President of the Federative Republic of Brazil and his wife walked into the crypt.

24 HOURS IN RAPPAHANNOCK

Don't blame John McCaslin, the editor of the Rappahannock News. He didn't ask me to write this, although he did publish it. I decided to write something about a few special things in Rappahannock County which we all know, but might forget to remember.

Like the dump. If you're looking to talk with some friends or just someone you know, drive to the dump at the Flatwood Mall. At least half the folks you know drive there every day just to chat, unless, of course, it's a Tuesday or Thursday. Do you know of a dump anywhere else that closes every Tuesday and Thursday? Last week we'd all heard that the truck they use to empty the trash bins had broken in half. That didn't cause anyone to stay home. Some of us just left our trash at home and came up to the Mall to talk about it. And it's the only dump in the world that doesn't smell too bad either, most of the year.

There's an alternative. If you walk or drive about a quarter mile north across Rte. 211 you come to Annie Williams' Mountainside Physical Therapy. Anyone over 60, or maybe 70, who isn't conversing at the Flatwood Mall will be there, even on Tuesday and Thursday. I've met a lot of friends there too, like Mayor Sullivan, or the Dietls or Cliff Miller, all being worked on by some of the most attractive therapists anywhere north of Brazil. Particularly great if you're as ancient as I am.

What you need after therapy is, of course, a tavern. We've got two of them. Headmasters in Sperryville and the Griffin in Flint Hill. They've got a new chef at Headmasters, and you'll be happy to hear that the rumors about Rachel leaving the Griffin Tavern are apparently wrong. She's still there and as far as I know, she has no plans to leave.

Or maybe VDOT blocked her escape from Flint Hill using the stop lights at Massey's Corner. We all know that there are no traffic lights in Rappahannock County. There are only those two flashing red lights where 522 and 211 intersect. You only see them if you are coming South from Flint Hill. So it's only half as bad as it might be. You don't see them if you are headed North, and there are no other lighted traffic signals of any kind anywhere in the County.

But what VDOT does, or doesn't do, with respect to stop lights, it makes up for with bridges. My favorite bridge sits in the grass beside the Copper Fox Distillery, across the parking lot from

Copper Fox Antiques. It has neither a stream nor a road passing underneath. It used to hold the road that passes over the Thornton River in Sperryville before VDOT built a new bridge there. The old bridge has seen better days, but I'm told some kids like to play on it.

For those of us, like me, who don't fix their cars themselves, we have three excellent garages:

Settles in Flint Hill, Shaws in Sperryville and B and B Service Center outside Sperryville. According to the County Surveyor's office, more than 50 of the cars in Rappahannock are parked in front of Shaws or next to the Thornton River, leaving only the remaining 49 to be divided between the other two garages. (Yes, I made that up, but it must be true.)

Talking about cars, until a month ago I didn't know that the speed limit through Woodville was only 35 mph. The sign is pretty far down the road towards Sperryville, and whenever I drove up 522 to Culpeper, as rarely as possible, I'd go barreling through the village at about 50 mph. Until a month ago.

I saw the blue and red lights flashing behind me before I even got through town. I stopped.

"What did I do wrong?" I asked the deputy.

"You were going 52 in a 35 mile per hour zone," she said.

"But I didn't see any sign," I said. That was true.

"It's right down there at the other side of town" she said. "Can I have your registration, please?"

She walked back to her car and got in, seeming to do

something on her radio. Then she walked back and stopped behind my car, and came to my open window. "I've got worse news," she said. "your registration has expired as well."

"Gosh," I gasped, " I didn't know that either."

She looked at me and scowled. "You'd better get that registration renewed quick," she said., "and watch the speed limit. We'll hammer you next time."

She handed me my expired registration card and walked back to her car. Finally she smiled.

"Have a nice day," she said, and then she drove away. Can you imagine that happening anywhere but in Rappahannock? It sure was a nice day.

Our police chief is pretty darn nice too. Connie is actually a member of the Lions Club, and if her time permits, she works with us behind the Co-op in the fall when the Lions are making apple butter. We've been doing it for years. After the apples are cut into quarters, we take them down to the centuries old canning facility in Keesletown. A couple of guys stay up all night long stirring those apples over the heat for some eight hours before they are spiced and sweetened and boiled up into apple butter. The next morning, at least a dozen more guys and women show up for steam cleaning and filling the jars and packing them up for the trip back to Rappahannock.

We sell them on the weekends outside Cookie's Shell gas station across from the neon-signed high school. Most of our customers don't know all the work that goes into making and selling a jar of apple butter. And it's good eating, too.

Before I end, I need to tell you a little about the theaters in Little Washington, the two of them, sort of catty-corner right down Gay Street from the court house and what used to be the jail.

Is there another town anywhere that has a population of about 170, with two working theaters? The two theaters get along just fine, thank you. And they don't really compete. One used to be a movie theater many decades ago, the other was once a church. One does a lot of music, the other a lot of plays. One has seats for an audience of 200, the other for roughly 110. Tickets at one are usually $25, at the other $15, sometimes free for kids. And they both get filled up on performance nights with people from all over the county or elsewhere.

Now, if you are a kind person, you could make both the editor and me happy by making believe that we have told you a fact or two that you didn't already know. Or maybe a couple of lies that you did. But all of this has been knocked off schedule by Covid-19. So you may have to wait awhile to see us perform. But I promise you we'll be back, if God and the County Board of Supervisors are willing to stick with us.

THE ETLAN GENERAL STORE

The old wooden building that once housed the Etlan General Store still stands on Route 231 in Etlan, Virginia, 90 miles southwest of the nation's capital, in the shadow of Old Rag Mountain. Like so many of the older buildings in Madison and Rappahannock counties, it has turned into an antique store where you can buy ceramics, old apple crates and rusted tools.

It wasn't that long ago, until 1984, that you could buy everything a local person could want at the Etlan General Store. You could buy nails and screws, paint and varnish, tools (not rusted), barbed wire, twine, nose rings for pigs, and any other hardware you could imagine. You could get canned goods, coffee, cold cuts, rat cheese, people cheese, Velveeta cheese, Coca-Cola, root beer, Dr. Pepper, bread, bologna, ham, lard, butter, milk, eggs, scrapple, potatoes and a few other things you wouldn't want to eat unless you were born in Etlan, VA. You could buy your clothes at the Etlan General Store - fuzzy flannel shirts, overalls, boots the soles' of which would never run thin, hats, hankies, men's underwear...but I don't think I ever saw a brassiere for sale, or panties either. Ruth may have kept these out of sight in the back. It wouldn't be decent to leave them in the glass cases out front.

Of course, there were cigarettes and snuff, a few cigars and penny candy, which the kids could pick themselves, out of the big glass case near the front of the store. And Zippo cigarette lighters and pocket knives, a few fish hooks, flies, some leader and some trout line. Christmas time there were oysters (used to sell about 75 gallons, Ruth said). And there was cracker meal to make a crispy crust when you fried 'em oystas in sizzling hot oil. Outside in the shed, Randolph had cement, sand, sand mix, fertilizer, fence posts, roof tar, shingles, tires (he'd fix yours if they were fixable).

If the Etlan store didn't have it, you didn't need it.

Except beer. Ruth's daddy, Dutton Yowell, who owned the place, didn't believe much in alcohol. If you had to have beer, you'd have to get it elsewhere. You weren't gonna buy it in his store. They had it at the grocery store cross the road. If you had to have beer, you could get it there.

Dutton owned maybe 300 acres just beyond the two stores

that were downtown Etlan. He bought the store in 1932 and ran it until his daughter Ruth and her husband, Randolph, and her sister Thelma, took it over in 1965. The store was open from 7:00 a.m. to 7:00 p.m. every day but Sunday, the 4th of July, Thanksgiving and Christmas.

There was never a time that I walked into that store and was greeted with anything other than an immense smile and "Well, look who's here. What d'ya need today, Peter?" And if you didn't have money with you, there was always credit. Not a credit card, store credit. The I.O.U.s were kept in a discreet wooden file box behind the counter. Sometimes, near the end of the month, the box got pretty full.

"Why do you bank all that?" I asked Ruth one time.

"Got to, Peter," she said. "People got to eat, and a lot of them only get paid end of the month. Usually they've gone through their money by then. So, we've got to give them credit or they wouldn't eat." Not many banks would do that for you.

Ruth was the postmistress. The government paid her $100 a month; she never asked for a raise. The post office looked a little like an old wooden phone booth, only a bit bigger. It stood near the front of the store. A little truck dropped off the mail for Etlan and Nethers early in the morning. Ruth would sort it, and then Ervin Weakley would deliver it to the mail boxes up and down valley and to the hollows that run up the edge of the Blue Ridge Mountains.

There was a pot belly stove in the back of the store, and

in the winter the old timers sat at a table close by and played cards. Ruth would cut them slabs of cheese for a nickel apiece. One time, one of the good ol' boys sent a healthy spit of tobacco into a trash basket.

"I could not have that," Ruth told me. "I told him he'd have to spit outside, no matter how cold it was. And after that, he did." Ruth wouldn't tell me who the guilty spitter was.

The best part of the store was the ice cream cooler. It greeted you when you came in the front screen door. There was vanilla, chocolate and strawberry, just like there should be. Ruth usually did the scooping. "How much is it?" I asked Ruth, the first time I bought a cone.

"5 cents, Peter," she said.

It was 1972. A nickel for an ice cream cone wasn't a bad deal, even then. And it wasn't a mean scoop either. The years went by, and a single scoop cone went up from a nickel to a dime. Then, sometime around 1978 or 1979, the price went up to 15 cents. Another year or two went by, and one day I walked into the store and the cooler was gone. Must be broken, I thought.

"What happened to the ice cream cooler?" I asked Ruth.

"Had it taken out," she said.

"But why?"

She sighed. "Peter, I just couldn't sell a cone for 15 cents a scoop anymore. I would have had to go up to a quarter. And 25 cents is too much for an ice cream cone. So I took it out."

Some years later I ran into Ruth at the Madison drug store

where she was working part time, and ordered an ice cream cone. It was 40 cents. I asked whether she remembered thinking that 25 cents was too much for a cone.

"Sure I do," she said. "And it was too much." I pointed out that she was now charging me 40 cents.

"That's too much, too," she said. But it ain't my store"

"Still is," Randolph said to me, about a week later, "No matter who owns it."

*****

Like I said, you could buy anything you needed at the Etlan General Store. Even a 1953 pickup truck, which I bought from Eddy Dyer.

Most any day, but especially on Saturdays, you could find a bunch of old timers sitting on the front porch (or, in the winter, around the wood stove in the back of the store). Most of them must have been in their 60's or 70's. Their names were Fincham, Jenkins, Lillard, Nicholson, Corbin, Weakley, Dodson, or Dyer, names of the families that had been pushed down out of the Blue Ridge Mountains in the 1930s to make way for the Shenandoah National Park.

Those who could afford it moved down into the hollows, as close to the mountains as they could get. Some of the old men who sat on the porch, smoking or drinking a Dr. Pepper (like I said, no beer at Dutton's) had grown up in the mountains before the Federal Government took their daddy's or granddaddy's land. They didn't have much use for the government, nor the Park Service either.

One Saturday in July I drove over to Etlan for some nails. The good ol' boys were out on the porch, as usual. Randolph was sitting with them, taking a short break. The Sheriff of Madison County, Hot Tinsley, an enormous man, was sitting with them, talking. Hot's actual name was H.O. Tinsley. In some past election, somebody ran his initials together and called him "Hot." Hot won, and the name stuck.

In front of the store was a 1953 Chevy pickup painted green, with a "For Sale" sign in the window. "Farm Use" was written in white paint on the tailgate in a none too steady hand.

"Whose truck is that," I asked.

Eddy Dyer raised one finger. "How much you want for it?" I asked. Eddy's eyes narrowed a little.

"$100 dollars," he said.

"How's it run," I asked.

"Engine runs good," Eddy said.

"If Peter buys it here," Randolph said to Eddy, "I get a 10% commission."

Everybody laughed.

"I'll take it," I said.

Eddy had been honest. The engine ran fine. But there were no brakes (or almost none), no clutch (really none), and the steering wheel turned 180 degrees before it began to turn the wheels. Kelsey Jones, who owned the Etlan junk yard down the road, worked on it for a couple days. We used our 1953 Chevy for the next seven years. I know Eddy was happy he'd unloaded his pile of junk metal on a city slicker for $100. But the city slicker was happy too.

In 1981 I moved to Brazil. I came back some years later and the store had closed. Ruth and Randolph had retired. Their daughter, Sheila, was living in what had been the store. We sat down on the porch.

"They just couldn't make a go of it anymore," she said. "You know, Daddy's getting older, and his arthritis was getting worse. Mom and Aunt Thelma were tired. Then there's Walmart over in Culpepper. They sell everything and a lot cheaper than we could do. You can't compete with them."

"They don't have a front porch," I said.

She laughed. "But the good ol' boys are dying off. Before long, there won't be anyone to sit on it."

"What about the credit your parents gave. Did they lose a lot when they closed?"

"It wasn't much," she said. "And most of it was owed by people who were dead. When they heard the store was closing, most all the alive ones came in and paid up, even those who couldn't afford it. I don't know where they got the money. The only big debt that never got paid was owed by a rich man over in Madison. He wouldn't even have felt it if he'd paid it off, but he never did."

"Same way with checks. Sure, a check bounced now and then. But they always made 'em good. There was only one check that never got paid, and that was from out of town. It was for $2.00."

"Suppose your grandfather had let the store carry beer?" I asked. "Do you think it would still be open?"

"I don't know," she said. "But you know, it wouldn't have been the same store. And we loved it just the way it was."

AT THE GEORGETOWN CLUB

The Friday Afternoon Drinking Society of the Georgetown Club was well into its second round of gin and ginger when Henry Witt pushed through the wooden swinging doors of the Common Room. The doors swung softly and closed behind him, shutting out the heat, the misery, and the poverty outside. Today the doors were especially welcome, for they shut out the corpse as well, the corpse that was propped by the kitchen gate, rotting in the sun.

Henry peered into the cavernous Common Room looking for his friends. He remembered when the room would have been full on a Friday afternoon, both in colonial times and later. But slowly they had begun to leave, the English first, and then, just as surely, many of the Guyanese: Bruce Kingman, Elton Persaud, Arrington Kennard, hundreds, then thousands more. They went to

Trinidad, to Barbados, to London, and Toronto.

And now, the Club on a Friday afternoon was all but empty. Henry waved to a couple of the boys in the "fish tank", the glassed-in enclosure where the Club's billiards addicts solemnly plied their sport in air-conditioned splendor. Beyond the fish tank, the massive wooden bar stood empty, as were the plastic covered tables and chairs, where the squash players, wringing wet after a "knock" in the tropical heat, were requested to sit, lest their perspiration forever defile the already frayed upholstery on the comfortable Berbice chairs. Overhead, an old wooden fan turned lazily in the heat of the afternoon.

Henry spotted the few remaining members of the Friday Afternoon Drinking Society sitting at a table next to the screen, near the end of the room. The Judge, as usual, was presiding, his long ebony fingers holding a cigarette with which he jabbed the airspace just under Isaac Nelson's mustache. Isaac had been the Police Commissioner before Independence, but neither this fact nor his fair skin and flaming red hair had been held against him when Independence came. He remained a member in good standing, though he was soon very much in a racial minority. Today, he and Henry were the only remaining Caucasian members of the Club. Isaac unquestionably had the finest mustache in Georgetown, a flaming red handlebar, and the right sort of temperament to go with it.

"What could I do?" the Judge was asking as Henry walked up. "She had seven pounds of onions! Seven pounds! Now one or two pounds she might have grown. But seven pounds? I simply had no choice."

The Judge looked up. "Oh look," he said, "It's Henry! Henry, we haven't seen you at our Friday afternoon drinking party in much too long. You work too hard, man. Come sit down, boy, come sit down. He clapped his hands smartly. "Chinee, Chinee," the Judge called out. "Mr. Witt will be needing a drink." He turned to Henry, "What will it be, boy?"

"A double demerara, please," Henry said. "I need one."

"Chinee," the Judge called out, "a double rum with coconut water, please, for my friend in need. In fact, better bring another round for us all." He chuckled. "I was just explaining to Cecil here about the onion case," said the Judge, resuming his more judicial demeanor.

The corpse buzzed through Henry's brain. But he couldn't interrupt the Judge in the middle of a story. It wasn't done. The Judge went on.

"This poor lady was arrested up in Mahaica, with seven pounds of onions. I don't know how the officer knew she had them, man, but she had them. Now the law makes an irrefutable presumption in the case of onions that they are contraband, and the penal code specifies the same penalty for all contraband: forfeiture, and minimum $30 or 30 days. Well she was a poor woman, and I just couldn't do it. Not for onions."

"So I violated the law. I gave her a good lecture about patriotism and sacrifice and all that rot, and fined her $10.00.

$10.00! My God the onions were worth more than that! Can you imagine what she said? She said she didn't have ten dollars, not for this Government even if she had it! So she'd rather do the thirty days, thank you very much. Thirty days!"

His long ebony fingers fluttered in the air like crows in flight, and then settled back to earth, interlocked over the gold chain, which adorned the vest, which covered the Judge's small potbelly.

"What did you do?" Isaac inquired.

"What else could I do," said the Judge. "I put her on probation. I couldn't put her in jail for possession of onions. It's not her fault, there are no onions in this benighted country, a shame. It's a rotten shame."

"What happened to her onions?" Isaac asked.

His eyes twinkling, as if he were about to reveal a wonderful secret, the Judge leaned close to Isaac, and belched. The smell of fried onions wafted into the Common Room.

"Corrupt bastard," said Isaac. Onions were his favorite food. He hadn't eaten any in years.

The Judge beamed. "Come for lunch tomorrow," he said.

"Lovable corrupt bastard," said Isaac. "I accept."

"12:15," The Judge then turned to Henry Witt and Cecil Williams. "Can you gentlemen join us tomorrow for lunch?" he inquired.

Williams was the Club President, a position he thoroughly enjoyed. "Ten years ago I couldn't walk into this club," he often told visitors, pointing to his brown skin. "Now I'm the President." He was a charter member of the Friday Afternoon Drinking Society, and hadn't missed a session in ten years. The Judge loved the arrangement, for Cecil Williams was a solicitor and gave the Judge a splendid foil for his Friday afternoon discussion of the week as seen from the bench.

But just now Williams was looking troubled. He either ignored the invitation, or hadn't heard.

"Look, Judge" he said, "how can you have an irrefutable presumption that onions are contraband? You know, and I know, that you can grow them almost anywhere. So how can the government make it an irrefutable presumption that they are unlawfully imported, and contraband? I say that's unconstitutional."

The Judge laughed. "Oh come, man. You know that the Government can do what it likes! If I decide that the presumption is refutable, it'll be my butt, with no re-butting permitted. All I can do is try to make the system a little more humane."

The Judge laughed, then turned serious. "Even that's not easy," he added, pointing up at the two official photographs on the wall. The one of the Prime Minister seemed to be smirking. The other, the Deputy Prime Minister, glowered behind his beard. They all knew the pictures well. They were posted on virtually every wall and telephone pole in Guyana.

Chinee arrived with the drinks and some cassava chips (potatoes were contraband too). Henry remembered his surprise when he had first met Chinee, some 20 years ago, and discovered that the barman wasn't Chinese at all, but East Indian. His official name was Ramrattan Singh, but nobody, including Chinee himself, ever used his official name. And nobody, including Chinee himself, could remember how, why, or when "Ramrattan Singh" became "Chinee".

In any case, he certainly didn't look Chinese. Just now, Chinee was looking very pleased to be seeing Henry again. "Welcome back, sir," he said. He headed back to the bar. "Long time no see," he added, with what passed for an oriental accent. Chuckling to himself over his joke, it seemed to Henry that his time had finally come. "Listen," he said, "there's a body..."

"5:30, Gentlemen," shouted the Judge. "5:30."

No one in the group looked the least surprised. For at that very moment, two aged gentlemen in mid-length tan Bermuda shorts, white hair, white skin, and plainly British, passed through the swinging doors, and marched over behind the screen. Once there, they snapped to attention and formally saluted the somewhat youngish photograph of H.R.H. Queen Elizabeth, which hung on the wall behind the screen. Duty done, they turned, and walked over to the bar for their rum swizzles, just as they had done every afternoon at precisely 5:30, ever since Independence. As one member of the Friday Afternoon Drinking Society had mentioned several years ago, you could set your watch by them.

"Could?" the Judge had said. "Let's do it!"

But when Independence came, the Judge had been as

happy as anyone to see the English go. But one of the things he had admired about the English was their punctuality. These days in Guyana if you asked a person to meet you at a particular hour, you were lucky if he showed up the next day. The Judge pulled his beautiful Victorian gold watch from his vest pocket. It was precisely 5:30. "Just right," chuckled the Judge, "just right."

"Well, Henry," said the Judge, finally turning to Henry Witt, "What's new man, what's new?"

Henry looked a great deal more somber than he usually did. Henry was a bush pilot, who flew his own small Cessna into the interior for whoever would pay him to do so. Often he returned to Georgetown sick with the hunger and suffering he saw inland. And on rare occasions, he drowned his sorrow in double Demeraras at the Club. But when he did that, he never flew. Henry refused to fly within 12 hours after he had taken alcohol. And since Henry needed to fly in order to live, late on Friday afternoons he generally drank his coconut water straight. But today he had finished his double Demerara in three gulps and was beckoning for Chinee to bring him another.

"Lord, Henry," said Isaac, "you must have seen something really God-awful out in the back country this time."

"Not in the interior," said Henry. "Right outside."

"Outside of where?" asked Cecil Williams.

"Here," said Henry. "In front of the Club. Near the corner."

Isaac and the Judge, both of whom were sitting by the

windows, looked out. There seemed to be nothing amiss. In front of the Club, a horse pranced by, pulling a long rubber-tired wooden cart, on which five or six boys had cadged a ride. From the muddy canal which ran down the middle of Camp Street over to the far side of the road, all was in order. From the Common Room windows you could not, however, see the area along the near side of Camp Street and around the corner into Lamaha Street, because of the wall which surrounded the Club.

"He's right there, hung up just beyond the wall."

"What do you mean, he?" said Isaac. "Who's he?"

"I'm glad," added the Judge, not unkindly, "that you do not fly your airplane with the same precision you employ in reporting on current events."

But the joke fell flat. Henry sighed. "I came in the service entrance," he said.

"You know, the one on Lamaha Street that smells so bad because of that sewer. But I was walking up Lamaha Street, and I decided to come in there because I was thirsty and didn't want to be late and there it was, hanging there. At least he looked like he was hanging there, as if someone had nailed him to those two telephone poles by his shirt."

Everyone knew where the two telephone poles were. Some three years ago, a young East Indian chap and his girlfriend had cut the corner at Lamaha and Camp Streets too short going about 40 miles an hour, and had crashed into the pole about 10 feet from the corner. They had come away unhurt, although their car had been demolished, and the pole had tipped over against the clubhouse, to a splendid display of sparks from the short circuited wires. Mr. Parkerson-Slough, the Club Secretary, had immediately called the fire brigade, but they had failed to come. About an hour later, they phoned to inquire whether they were still needed. Since no one answered, the Fire Brigade had assumed the place had burned down, and had gone back to their dominos.

Fortunately, however, the clubhouse had not burned down. In fact, it hadn't caught fire at all. And after examining all aspects of the accident, the members had all returned upstairs for a round of drinks together before returning to their respective corners of the Club.

With remarkable dispatch, the Guyana Electricity Corporation, within 10 days, planted a new pole next to the old one, connected the two poles with a piece of barbed wire, and winched the old pole up to where it leaned only four or five feet from the vertical.

Since that time no further action had been taken, whether to transfer the wires onto the new pole, or to remove the old one. So the two poles stood there, lashed together by barbed wire, about six feet above the ground, waiting for the next couple who would cut the corner too close.

"What do you mean, he was hanging, Henry?" the Judge asked, serious now. "You mean by the neck?" His Honor had some difficulty when words he felt to be proper legal terminology were used by a layman with imprecision.

"No, Judge. He rather looks as if someone had fished him out of the canal and hung him out to dry."

"Maybe he's just a drunk, and someone's played a trick," the Judge said, his long black fingers waking from their nap on his belly and sailing into the air. "Are you sure the man is dead?"

"I didn't really look that closely," said Henry. But he didn't look very lively...And he sure didn't smell good."

"But could that not have been the sewer?" the Judge asked. The thing about private practice he missed most was cross-examination. Henry shrugged.

"I think he was dead," he said.

"Do you have any idea who he was?"

"His head was hanging down," said Henry. "But I don't think I've ever seen him before, unless maybe, sometime, long ago. He sure didn't smell good." he added.

It was just then that Chinee interrupted. "Your Honor," he said.

The Judge did not like the interruption.

"Excuse me?" asked Chinee, politely.

"Oh," said the Judge. "Excuse me, you're overruled," he said. Then somewhat more kindly, "What is it, Chinee?" Chinee set down his tray of drinks.

"Excuse me," Chinee said again, "are you gentlemen speaking of the man who's hanging down there by the service entrance?"

"Yes, we are," said Cecil.

"Well," said Chinee. "That fellow was down there all day yesterday, and he didn't look none too healthy then."

At first no one spoke, then all of them began to speak at once. The Judge took an empty beer stein which he employed, to good advantage, as a gavel. Everyone quieted down.

"We clearly must send a commission to investigate," he said. "To identify the body, if a body it is. And you," he said to the well-dressed young man sitting next to Cecil Williams, "You, Isaac, on the strength of your extensive experience as Police Commissioner, will be the chairman. You, Henry, must go along. You, Benjamin, must go along to run and summon the constabulary in case of need. Now I myself shall hold the fort here. For one, the matter may yet wind up before me in Court. I shouldn't be directly involved. Besides, I haven't finished my last drink."

The Judge looked around the group, his eyes lighting on Cecil Williams. He knew how Williams hated to look upon violence and death. Cecil was a very gentle man. "Cecil, you must remain here with me, in case a need should arise. And anyway," he whispered, "who likes to drink alone?"

Isaac Nelson, his mustache more bristly than ever, stood up, almost to attention. "Alright troops," he said with a grin, "let's go." But it was plain that all of them were taking it seriously. Isaac and his platoon marched through the swinging doors, and out of sight down the stairs.

"What now?" asked Cecil.

"Now," said the Judge, "we wait for a report. We wait for a report, and we drink."

The Judge leaned back in his Berbice chair, his own personal pillow behind his head, and closed his eyes. Almost. Through just a slit, he looked out the window at the place in the wall where the two poles stuck up like rabbit ears, as if by narrowing his eyes he could see right through the damnable wall. The Judge pushed his chair back a little further, until it bumped the screen. That screen went back to colonial times.

One of the younger members of the Membership Committee, apparently under some pressure from his wife, had proposed that women be permitted to join the Club. The Committee roundly defeated the proposal, but the Club did recommend to the Rules Committee that it consider whether the Rules should be modified to permit ladies to visit the Common Room at specified hours. The meeting of the Rules Committee had been stormy, with old Mr. Parkerson-Slough leading the defenders of the status quo.

"If we let them in the Common," he cried, "they'll soon be in the Dining Hall, or even in the bedrooms upstairs!"

He was right, of course, on both counts, but most of the Committee knew by then that as difficult as ladies could be at times, on the whole, life was more enjoyable with them than without them. And the notion of ladies in the bedrooms on the third floor had given more than one member a delicious tingly feeling. A motion was made, seconded, and carried that ladies be admitted to the Common Room, but that they be required to sit on the far side of a screen, to be placed crosswise, fifteen-feet from the end of the room, so that those who didn't like ladies wouldn't have to look at them. Old Parkerson-Slough had fainted. Although the screen had lost its original purpose several years ago, it had never been removed. Now, in fact, it served to protect that most notable of all ladies, H.R.H. Queen Elizabeth. When Independence came, her photograph had been moved behind the screen: where no one who didn't care to would have to look at her.

"There goes Benjy," said Williams. Outside, Williams' young assistant had already turned the corner out of Lamaha Street, and was loping up Camp Street towards the police barracks.

"Yes, there he goes." said the Judge. Then they both settled back to wait. But at that moment, the cacophony went off, defiling the stillness of the late afternoon. It sounded as if beginners' Bugle class of the Georgetown Club was rehearsing 15 feet away.

In fact, that was precisely what it was. Several years before, the ruling Peoples National Congress (PNC) had purchased the Victorian mansion next door to the Club, and had there installed the party secretariat. The Party Secretary thought it would be a splendid idea to hold rehearsal sessions in the garden each evening, at an hour when he would be comfortably ensconced drinking contraband whiskey in his rather elegant house several miles away, in Kitty. Not only was it a fine place to practice, thought the Secretary, but the noise would be sure to drive those reactionaries next door crazy.

At first, it had done just that, but since the PNC controlled the Government, there was little the Club could do. When Cecil, as Club president, had gone next door to plead for a little consideration, a charming youth had stuck his trumpet in Cecil's ear and blown so hard that he had been unable to hear for a week. But as with most curses, the Club had, in time, grown used to the racket. Indeed, the Judge hardly heard it any more, after the first few butchered notes.

"Oh, no," the Judge shouted, above the din. "Thrushbottom."

Cecil peered out the window, and nodded. Coming down Camp Street on his bicycle, Benjy jogging alongside him, came Constable Eustace Thrushbottom, the enormous cheeks of his backside ballooning out on either side of the tiny bicycle seat.

"The only thing Thrushbottom's bottom has in common with a thrush," the Judge had once commented, "is its probable color."

The Judge was a great believer in precision in language. He was not about to make a statement that could be interpreted as indicating that he might actually have seen the Constable's bottom. Now he merely sighed. "That man can figure out more reasons not to do something than any man I know," he said to Cecil. "I'll bet nothing happens."

He was right. The Constable was not five minutes out of

sight behind the wall when he emerged again, looking more grumpy than was usual even for him, and pedaled off down Camp Street. The swinging doors of the Common Room slammed open, and Isaac strode through, followed by Henry Witt and Benjamin. The former police commissioner was at least as red as his mustache. And the mustache quivered.

"That lazy son-of-a-bitch," he shouted. "I should have fired him when I still had the chance!"

"That's true," said the Judge gently. "But you didn't. That was long ago, Isaac. No use crying now over un-spilt milk...or blood."

"Eustace Thrushbottom..." Isaac sputtered. "Eustace, hell. His name should be 'Useless', not 'Eustace'! He wouldn't do a God damn thing!"

"I suspect," said the Judge quietly, "that if all of our public officials were to follow Useless's example, we would all be better off." His index finger seemed to fly across the room, snag Chinee's attention, and direct it at Isaac, whose color was slowly receding from that of a boiled lobster back to more human tones.

"What happened?" the Judge asked Henry.

"Well," said Henry, "it's just as Isaac said. Thrushbottom came down and looked around the body for a minute or two. He never even took it down, or took off any of its clothes. Nonetheless, after maybe two minutes of investigation, he announced that he could see no evidence of foul play, and that this was not, therefore, a case for the constabulary. Moreover, he said, it was time for his dinner." Henry paused for a moment, then added, "But what really got to Isaac was his final comment." He motioned for no one to ask the obvious question until Chinee could arrive with another drink for Isaac.

"What did he say?" Cecil asked. Cecil always asked the obvious question, that was part of the reason the old Judge loved him. Fortunately, Chinee had already arrived with a double rum and coconut water and Isaac was looking almost composed.

Henry waited until his old friend had taken two long draws on his drink. "He said that he thought at least some members of the party would have had the intelligence to call the ambulance, rather than needlessly disturbing the hardworking Cooperative People's Constabulary with this sort of tomfoolery." Isaac's color darkened dangerously, and Henry paused until Isaac had drained his glass. The Judge waited in rapt attention. "Just before he left," Henry went on, "the Constable added that of course today's Constabulary was of a substantially higher level of intellect than the fools who ran the force in colonial times."

There was a crash and the sound of broken glass falling at the PNC Secretariat next door. And then silence. Isaac had flung his empty glass, full force, out the window. It had shattered against the soil stack of the building next door showering glass, ice and a bit of lemon rind on the heads of the Peoples Cooperative Drum and Bugle Corps - Beginners Section, out in the yard. The God-awful noise stopped.

The Friday Afternoon Drinking Society sat in silence, not

really realizing what it was that was different, but knowing that something was definitely, most pleasantly, different. It wasn't until one of the trumpeters tried a tentative bleat that they realized what was different. The silence. The blessed silence. Then there was another bleat, and a drum made a sound something like a file being rubbed over the snares.

The Judge picked up his glass and drained the last drops. Then he silently handed it to his friend. Isaac grinned, reared back, and fired the glass through the window, hitting the soil stack again. Again the sound of the falling glass was followed by silence. But this silence had a ring of permanence about it.

"Bravo! Well done, Isaac," shouted the Judge, his face beaming.

"A round of drinks for everyone, Chinee. Yes, old Ballsgrave and Cocksworthy, too," he said, pointing at the two ancient Englishmen. "Isaac, that's the best pitching I've seen you do since the Constabulary played the Judiciary down at the Georgetown Cricket Club way back when." Now they all began to talk, and congratulate Isaac on his formidable right arm. Ballsgrave and Cocksworthy came over, as did Chinee, and they all forgot about the man hanging on the barbed wire downstairs, until Henry said, "What about the guy on the wire?"

They all stopped. "I wonder if he's still there," said Williams.

His disappearance didn't seem very likely, but it was worth a try. Benjamin was dispatched to go and check. The man was, of course, still there.

"Well, what now?" asked Henry.

It was Chinee who broke the silence. "Perhaps we should call an ambulance," he said. The others, of course, had thought of the same idea, but as this had been Thrushbottom's suggestion, they understandably feared that to second it might cause the next flying glass to be targeted at them. Isaac's temper had, however, cooled. It took two minutes now that he was back among friends. Moreover, he had a genuine affection for Chinee and his common sense intelligence.

"Good idea," he said, as if Chinee had been the first to think of it. "Could you ring the Fire Brigade..." Isaac paused, remembering the last time the Fire Brigade had been called, several years ago. "No, Chinee, don't call the Fire Brigade. Call the Georgetown Hospital, would you please. And ask them to send an ambulance right away. The hospital's so close, they should be here in three minutes. And Chinee, something seems to have happened to my glass. And to the Judge's too. Would you bring two more please...and put some gin and ginger in them. After all," he added to his friends, "nature abhors a vacuum."

It took the ambulance exactly an hour to arrive. The hospital was close enough down Lamaha Street that they could hear the siren start up when it left the hospital 58 minutes (timed on the Judge's pocket watch) after Chinee called. This time, Cecil Williams and Benjamin were dispatched to deal with the visitors. But the ambulance remained even more briefly than the

55

Constable, before it slid away. Cecil and his assistant returned upstairs with a heavy step. "He's dead," said Cecil, his usually warm brown face now tinged greenish-grey.

"They got out of the ambulance," Benjamin reported, "and went straight to the body. One of them shoved a stethoscope inside his clothes and listened, and the other one held a mirror under his nose. Then one of them said, 'You are wasting our time. This man needs an undertaker, not an ambulance!' And then they drove away."

"Hell, at least they came," said the Judge wearily, remembering the Fire Brigade.

"Excuse me, please, my friends," said Cecil, who now looked totally grey. He sprinted for the men's room. The sounds he made there were almost enough to make Isaac regret that he had silenced the PNC Drum and Bugle Corps. But when he emerged, Cecil looked a great deal better, and his skin color was back to a healthy brown. Everyone waited for the Judge to speak.

"I suppose," said the Judge, "that the ambulance driver had a point. If the man is truly dead, there is no solution but to call J.Q." The man to whom the judge was referring was, they all knew, J.Q. Applespith, Embalmer, Undertaker and Master of the Funereal Arts (as his advertisement in the Georgetown Daily Mirror read).

There were other undertakers in Georgetown, but none of the others had a real motorized hearse. Moreover, the Judge knew old J.Q. from the early days, before capital punishment had been abolished, and J.Q. had doubled as hangman for Georgetown and East Coast Demerara. In a number of cases, the Judge and J.Q. had worked together, so to speak, to ensure that some scoundrel murderer, child molester, or rapist would no longer terrorize the women and children of Guyana. Ever. "Chinee," said the Judge, "Go call Mr. J.Q. Applespith please, and ask him to bring his hearse around right away. We have some business for him...and oh, Chinee, there's no need to tell J.Q. who the body is."

"No sir," said Chinee, "In fact, sir, begging your pardon, Your Honor, but we don't know who it is, do we?"

"That's true, Chinee, but there's no need to tell him that either." With one long black finger, the Judge waved Chinee in the direction of the phone. Outside, the afternoon had turned to dusk, in five or ten minutes it would be pitch dark. "The man who invented the phrase 'nightfall'" the Judge once said, "must have lived in the tropics." In Guyana, it fell with an almost audible thud. Now the Judge looked around at his friends.

"It won't take old J.Q. long", he said. We'd better drink up, and go down." None of them looked anxious to go. "Come on," he said. "Let's all go. I haven't seen old J.Q. in months. Besides, it doesn't look like a possible court case after all. At least that's what the Constable said."

"Good night, Chinee, and thanks," he called to the barman. The Judge drained his glass, and stood up. "Come on," he said, and without weaving (well, almost without weaving) he walked to the swinging doors.

Isaac, Henry, Cecil and Benjamin followed the Judge down the stairs. It was his favorite hour, to the West tropical clouds billowed high and purple in the gathering dusk, promising a thunderstorm before morning. In the church yard across the way, a chickadee was singing "chickadee, chickadee, chickadee." It sounded a little mournful. The Judge paused at the door, took a deep breath of the tropical air, then turned, and as if he had given himself an order, marched to the corner of Lamaha Street. There he turned and walked to the two poles.

The body hung there, just as Henry had described, the head drooped forward, making it difficult to see the face. A small dirty cap covered some of the hair. The Judge's long fingers, even blacker now against the pallor of the corpse, lifted the head so that he could see the face.

He did not know the face, yet he had seen it a thousand times, in the streets, in the sugar cane fields where he had worked as a child, in his courtroom. It seemed to contain a little of each of Guyana's races, which in life held themselves so separate from one another, even in the villages where they lived. The features were a little like the Judge's own assistant, with broad lips and nose. But the hair was east Indian - straight, thick, and black - under the dried-on mud and slime from the canal. His complexion seemed to have been almost white, before it acquired the green-grey pallor of death. And finally the eyes, mercifully closed now, looked just the slightest bit slanted. The Judge stared. Then he let the face fall back onto the body's chest.

At that moment, a large black vehicle clanked and backfired its way around the corner from Camp Street, coughed, and pulled up next to them. It was, of course, J. Q. Applespith's hearse. "A hearse," the Judge once said, "should glide."

J.Q.'s hearse most definitely did not glide. Indeed it was a miracle that it ran at all, given that automotive parts, like onions and potatoes, were irrefutably contraband. The hearse was, however, black, ambulatory (barely) and on the door was painted, in red stick-on letters, flecked with gold:

* J.Q. APPLESPITH *
* FUNERALS OF DISTINCTION *

The selfsame Applespith opened the door and got out. "Your Honor," he cried "what a pleasure to thee you. J.Q. Applethpith, at your servith. Who ith the poor loved one who ith patht on along God'th way?"

The Judge had quite forgotten that J.Q. had a lisp. Poor J.Q. had strayed too close to a wretch he had hanged several years ago, and in his death throes, the fellow had kicked out two of J.Q.'s front teeth. The result was that J.Q. now lisped and he sprayed everyone with whom he spoke with a fine mist of rum and saliva. He had particular accuracy with the hard "T".

In fact, he had succeeded in getting the Judge in the eye twice in the course of his initial greeting. J.Q. was now looking carefully at the members of the Friday Afternoon Drinking

Society, but they all looked quite alive, although Cecil looked a little green. And on the ground, there was no corpse to be seen.

The Judge pulled from his pocket a linen handkerchief (a gift from a merchant on Regent Street years before), and wiped his face. He backed a respectful distance from the undertaker, and pointed to the man hanging between the poles. "There he is, J.Q. but to tell you the God's honest truth, he's not really a 'loved one' of any of us, not in the usual sense. We've all seen him a thousand times, though we have never seen him before."

J.Q. looked at the Judge as if he had had too much to drink, but being a judge and an old friend, was nonetheless entitled to respect. Then he stared at the mud-caked body. "That'th what you want me to take?" he asked. "That? Doeth anybody know who it wath?"

No one spoke.

"Well, I'm damned if I'll take him," said Applespith heatedly. "It'll be another indigent burial ordered by the Government for $200! But they don't pay! You know how much the Government oweth me now for indigent burialth? $8,200! $8,200!" he screamed. "You know how many bodieth that ith? That'th 41 stiffth! I thwore I wouldn't do it any more for free and I won't. Not until those fuckerth pay up. Not even for you, Judge," he said, looking fondly at his former colleague, "but I'll take old Williamth there if you like."

No one laughed. J.Q. Applespith turned and got back in his hearse.

"I'm thorry," he said, "I'm really thorry."

"But what are we to do with him?" Isaac asked the undertaker. "I don't know," said Applespith, "I don't know. If you'd acted a little thooner, maybe the ambulanth would have taken him. But not thith way, the way he lookth now. Maybe the polith...Well, I'm thorry," he said again. And then he drove away.

"What did he mean by that wisecrack about me?" Cecil asked.

"Oh, he was just making a joke," said the Judge. "You do look a little green. Maybe you'd better go home to your lady fair."

"Yes, well perhaps so," said Cecil. "It is getting late." He paused, "Well, good night, friends," he said.

"Actually, can I get a ride with you?" Isaac asked.

"Sure," said Cecil. "Benjy, you'll be needing a ride as well, won't you?"

There was another round of goodbyes, and then they were gone, leaving the Judge and Henry with the body. They stood silently, watching a few lights flicker along Camp Street. Then the Georgetown light house, down on Water Street, came on, signaling the arrival of night.

"I'm afraid I've got to go too," Henry said to the Judge. "I'm due in Port Kaituma tomorrow at 9:00. I may have to bend my 12 hour rule as it is."

"I grant you judicial dispensation," said the Judge. "Fly safely. I need you at the Friday Afternoon Drinking Society more often."

Henry smiled. "Thanks," he said. "Good night, Judge. And be careful yourself. You know how the choke and rob boys like things after dark."

"Don't worry, Henry," said the Judge. "But make sure to come next Friday afternoon to check if I'm still alive."

"I will," said Henry, "God willing. Good night."

The Judge stood silently in front of the two poles. Someone upstairs at the Club had turned on a few lamps, one of which cast a dim stream of light onto the body. As the Judge watched, a large fly buzzed over the corpse's head, and landed on its nose.

"Poor country," he said, "poor, poor country."

Taking his linen handkerchief from his pocket, he carefully brushed the fly away. He started to put the handkerchief back into his pocket, then stopped. Very slowly, he lifted the peak of the corpse's hat with his right hand, while with the fingers of the left, he placed the handkerchief carefully over the face. Then, he pulled the cap back down so that the handkerchief remained in place. The shroud rippled a little in the warm evening breeze. The Judge looked somewhat nervously over his shoulder.

There was no one there.

THE GAROTA DE IPANEMA

My old friend Paulo Rocha and I sat on the terrace of the Rio de Janeiro Sheraton, just beyond where the Ataulfo de Paiva canal marks the end of Leblon. It was dark now, and an occasional flicker of tropical lightning danced above the islands several kilometers out to sea. We could hear the gringos laughing inside the bar of the hotel. A Muzak version of "The Girl from Ipanema" blared much too loud from inside. "I can't write about Brazil in the lobby of the Sheraton," I groused to Paulo.

"Come," he said. "Let's have a walk down the beach. What you need is a good Brazilian *caipirinha*. Come on."

We walked down past the favela slum at Vidigal. "Can you make it as far as Ipanema?" Paulo asked, grinning.

I nodded, "Yes."

"I'll take you to the Garota de Ipanema bar," Paulo said,

"It's only a block from the beach." It was just an ordinary bar with an ordinary clientele until Antônio Carlos Jobim and his friend Vinicius de Morais started meeting there in the late afternoon to drink their *caipirinhas* and talk about music and girls. Antônio Carlos was a composer, Vinicius was a diplomat who cared much more for poetry than for international politics. His poetry seemed to fit perfectly with Jobim's music. They called it *'bossa nova'*, the 'new way'. Pedro Luis, the owner of the bar and no fool, set aside a small table and some chairs for them in the back corner of the bar and wrote 'Tom Jobim' and 'Vinicius' on the wall behind their table. Before long, young people began to congregate in the bar late in the afternoon to hear Jobim practicing Bossa Nova on his guitar and listening to Vinicius's poetry that provided the lyrics for Jobim's music.

"Perhaps the most successful," Paulo continued, "was a song about a beautiful young woman who walked by the bar on her way to the beach, but never stopped to talk to the young man in the bar who silently watched her go by. He loved her, but she didn't even see him or care that he was there. Vinicius wrote some wonderful lyrics for the song. They decided to call it 'A Garota de Ipanema' - The Girl from Ipanema. It was a tremendous success." Pedro Luis renamed his bar with the name of the song. Like I said, he was no fool. Today you can hear it in the lobby of the Sheraton and a thousand other places in the world.

We turned left, away from the beach and walked down to the bar. On the sidewalk next to the newly whitewashed walls, there were three street musicians carrying a guitar, a tambourine and a small drum, playing a song from the Brazilian Northeast. They stopped playing to greet Paulo and give him an *abraço*.

"They're old friends," Paulo said "Let's find us a table."

One of the waiters came rushing over. "Paulo, how good to see you. Who is your friend?"

"His name is Peter," Paulo said, "He's an American, but he speaks good Portuguese." He turned to me. "This is José, best waiter in the whole South Zone." José Antônio beamed.

"Come in, come in," he said in Portuguese, "and I'll bring you the best *caipirinha* in Ipanema." He showed us to a table by the window where the musicians were playing just outside.

"What's the small guitar called?" I asked Paulo.

"It's called a *bandolim*," he said. "You need it if you are going to play country music from the Northeast. It's nothing like Jobim's music, but it's pure Brazilian. They make up the lyrics as they go along."

I looked over at the names on the wall. "Who is Tom Jobim?" I asked. "I thought his name was Antônio Carlos."

Paulo shrugged. "It is," he said, "I have no idea why we call him 'Tom'. The foreigners call him 'Antônio Carlos'. We Brazilians call him Tom."

"Is he still alive?" I asked.

"Vinicius died three years ago," Paulo said. "Tom is still alive but I hear he is very sick. He is in a hospital in New York. That reminds me, I really must go home for dinner or my wife will put me in the hospital too." He got up. "Anyway it looks like it's going to rain. Um *grande abraço*, my friend. I'll call you tomorrow." He gulped down the last drop of his *caipirinha* and was out the door. José Antônio hurried over to pick up his empty glass.

"He's gone home," I said.

"How about another *caipirinha* for you," José Antônio asked.

A *caipirinha* is the Brazilian national drink made of crushed chunks of green lemon, sugar, ice and Brazilian *cachaça*, the Brazilian white lightning rum that is usually 80 or 100 proof. The *caipirinha* I had just finished was indeed one of the best I had ever tasted.

"Why not?" I said.

José Antônio scurried away. "Be right back," he said.

I looked down the row of tables that looked out the open windows to the street. There were four Brazilian men sitting at the table next to mine talking about soccer. Two of them were wearing red and black striped shirts, the other two were dressed in green and black. They were talking about the annual Fluminense vs. Flamengo soccer game, better known as the Fla-Flu, between Rio's two best professional teams scheduled for the next night. The rivalry between the fans of the two teams is fierce and could even give way to violence.

The guys at the next table were clearly friends but the discussion among them was a bit hostile. One of the red and black

shirted guys leaned over toward my table, "What do you think?"
he asked. I decided it would be wiser to pretend that I didn't speak
Portuguese. I just shrugged. At the next table were only two
drinkers, an American sailor and a heavily made up Brazilian girl.
The sailor clearly didn't speak Portuguese and the girl didn't
speak at all. Under the table she was stroking his navy blue pants
and fiddling with the zipper. The sailor was obviously smitten by
the girl. She looked bored.

The couple sitting at the next table over seemed to be
German tourists, perhaps 70 years old. They were drinking
'chopp' as Brazilian draught beer is called, and not talking to each
other. They were the only ones in the bar who did not seem to be
having a good time, perhaps because they did not approve of the
girls sitting at the table next to them, or perhaps because they were
German.

On one side were the sailor and the pretty woman. On the
other side there were four young prostitutes drinking caipirinhas.
I knew one of them, but very indirectly. She seemed to have an
inside track with the night desk clerk at the Sheraton who, for a
small fee, would arrange female company for guests at the hotel
if they wanted. I would occasionally cross with her in the elevator
late at night or early in the morning when she was headed for the
ground floor. Her name was Mariazinha. The other three were all
flowers, Lily, Rosinha and Violeta. Mariazinha waved to me
across the bar.

It was just about then that a gigantic lightning bolt flashed down out of the sky and into the building across the street. A torrent of rain came coursing down the awnings over the windows. A tremendous crack split the air, then a roar of thunder seemed to shake the building to its roots. The lights went out and the four young prostitutes at the last table were screaming.

José Antônio, who had been hiding behind the bar, came rushing over with a flashlight to close the windows. "What rain," he said, "I never saw anything like this in my life." He hurried over to the next table.

I looked out the window. You could barely see the building across the street through the rain. All the street lights and those in the buildings across the street were out. It was pitch black, except for a small white light and an occasional flicker of red moving up and down as it slowly came down the street toward the bar. I was the first one to see it.

I called José over. "What's that?" I asked him.

"I have no idea," he said.

By this time all of the customers in the bar had seen it, the girls stopped screaming and sat frozen with fear, looking up Rua Vinicius de Moraes towards the sea. "Just stay quiet until we know what it is," Mariazinha said. No one argued.

The lights slowly moved closer until we could see that it was a black bicycle coming down the street toward the bar. There were small red lights attached to the pedals and two white lights on the handlebars. Riding it was a figure in a black skin-tight suit with a white skeleton painted on the back of it, a black mask, and black shoes. The bicycle seemed to be towing a long wooden box that looked like a coffin with two small green lights on the rear. The skeleton waved slowly toward the bar.

"It's death!" Rosinha screamed, "it's death!", and burst into tears.

By this time, everyone in the bar was screaming. The figure on the bike looked over at the bar and grinned. His teeth were yellowed. Mariazinha had been studying the box behind the bicycle. She walked over to my table.

"Look," she said "there's a red and black striped cloth over the box. That's the flag of Flamengo. It's not a box, it's a coffin. I'll bet there's a Fluminense flag inside."

I looked out the window at the black figure. "You mean it's a symbol that says Flamengo is going to come out on top."

"Sure," she said. "It looks like Death, but it's not. We do some of those images in my profession. It feels like love, if you do it right. One of my customers said it's a metaphor. What does that mean?"

"I have no idea," I said, "Maybe it's like The Girl from Ipanema. The boy loves her but love doesn't really exist."

"Oh," Mariazinha said. But she still looked a little puzzled. I looked out the window just in time to see the biker peddling off into the rain.

The lights came on again ten minutes later. The rain stopped about a quarter hour after that. José brought free *caipirinhas* for everyone, explaining Mariazinha's theory to them and that it had to be right.

I didn't leave the bar until after eleven o'clock. The clock on the wall of the building across the street was stopped at 10:13 p.m., the time the lighting had struck. I looked for the names of Jobim and Vinicius that had been painted on the wall. The table was there but I couldn't find the names. "What happened to the names on the wall," I asked José Antônio.

He looked at me strangely. "What names?" he said.

I woke up at the hotel at 8 o'clock the next morning. The *Jornal do Brasil* was waiting outside my door. "Tom is dead," the headline shouted. He had died in the hospital in New York at 10:13 p.m. Rio time the paper said. There would be a national day of mourning.

And Flamengo had won.

THE CAFE

Americans tend to think of Zurich as a railroad station, to be passed through as quickly as possible on the way to Geneva or Zermatt. Others think it is a city of a thousand banks at which half the world secretly keeps its money. Maybe so.

But my story is not about Zurich, nor even the Zurichers. It is rather about a small cafe that for a time happened to be located in Zurich, up on the hill on the left bank of the Limmat River which divides the city down the middle. The left bank, down near the river, holds the "bohemian" section of town (albeit more Greenwich Village than Bohemia itself). On up the hill there are quiet, tree-lined streets, the magnificent Zurich Art Museum (although you wonder, sometimes, about the true past of the pieces), and a charming small hotel, run by a young Swiss couple, which they call the "Shapirohof". The Americans love it, the Swiss don't get it.

Susan and I arrived in Zurich in March 2003, on one of those mornings that was no longer winter, but not yet spring. We had not had much sleep. The train from Zermatt, which takes roughly five hours and requires four transfers, had left Zermatt at 5:00 a.m. We arrived in Zurich at 9:47 a.m., precisely on time, and took a taxi to the Shapirohof. Max Shapiro greeted us effusively, but apologetically. Our reservation was, of course, in order, but check-out time was 12:00 noon and the preceding guest hadn't yet left. Unfortunately, breakfast was over and the breakfast chef had gone home. But could he offer us a cup of coffee? Or would we prefer to go out to a cafe at the hotel's expense? In any case, the room would be certainly ready at 12:25 p.m. We opted to seek out a cafe, although we declined Max's generous offer to pick up the bill. "Well, we'll make you a special lunch," said Max. "But please be here by 12:30 p.m." I promised we would.

The street in front of the hotel heads sharply down the hill, crosses another tree-lined street where the trees were just beginning to bud, and ends at a somewhat larger avenue which runs across the hill. The number 6 tram - a sleek, perfectly kept red trolley - rolled smoothly down the middle of the avenue. Susan and I turned right and walked down toward a sign which said simply "Cafe". We stopped and looked in. There was a lace curtain over the window, and it was difficult to see inside. But it looked like the sort of quiet, old-fashioned place we like, particularly after five hours on the train. We went in.

The cafe from the inside lived up to its outside promise. It was old, quite dark, and very European. The walls were yellowed by years of cigarette smoke, and a hint of a Gauloise hung in the air. On the back wall were a few photographs of the Alps, in small wooden frames. We were the only customers, other than an old gentleman with white hair and a Swiss loden jacket, sleeping peacefully in one of the booths along the back. There were other booths along the street side, each with its own lace-curtained window, which gave the place a filtered light. On the right was a counter bearing a large old copper espresso machine. A tray full of demitasse cups sat next to it, together with the obligatory "apfelkuchen". A large yellow tabby lay on the floor next to a small coal-burning stove.

"This is great," I said to Susan. "Just like the cafes in my student years. The old ones from before the war." Susan nodded and smiled.

A woman's voice came from behind us, soft and gentle, with only a slight touch of a German-Swiss accent. "Sit wherever you like," she said. She emerged quietly out from the shadows at the back of the cafe, a slim gray-haired woman, perhaps in her late 50s, with gray, somewhat tired eyes that looked as if they once had laughed, but did so no more. Her dress was also gray, and came well below her knees.

"You are Americans," she said, not as a question, but a simple statement of fact.

And then, "What can I get you?"

"Zwei grosse braune," I said, disporting my best German. "Und vier croissant."

She smiled and walked over to an empty table bearing a small basket. She took the basket to the next table, where she dumped the contents of the first basket into the second, and brought the basket of four croissants back to our table. "So," she said, as if to say, "there" or "voila" and walked over to the espresso machine. Her back was to us, and we could not tell exactly what she was doing. But the machine did a good deal of gurgling and hissing, and a few moments later, she brought over two "grosse braune", large cups of espresso coffee turned a golden brown by the steaming milk. She silently put two small glasses of water and a copy of Zurich's famed newspaper, the *Zuricher Nachrichten*, on our table, and disappeared into the kitchen.

It had begun to snow, and we settled into our booth warmed by the little coal stove, very pleased with ourselves for having found a wonderfully European old cafe. The coffee was delicious, and we sipped it slowly to make it last. The croissants were crisp and buttery. The world was peaceful and good.

But the peace did not last long. A metallic clanking and clattering sound was coming down the avenue, growing louder as it came.

"Look," said Susan. "It's one of the old trams, like San Francisco. It must be for tourists. Look at the bell!"

Above the red and black body of the tram, there was a

gleaming brass bell, and the driver reached up and pulled the cord and rang it as the tram stopped outside the cafe. The only passenger, a rotund individual, jumped from the tram, waved to the driver and walked quickly across the avenue into the cafe. The tram rumbled off down the hill, and disappeared into the swirling snow, as its former passenger emerged through the heavy green blankets which hung ceiling to floor, inside the outer door of the cafe, to keep the heat inside when the door was opened.

"Freddo," he shouted, "molto freddo," and he slapped his large hands around his expansive torso, while jumping up and down with surprising agility. The whole performance wakened the old man who had been sleeping in the back.

"Bongiorno, Herr Franz!" shouted the boisterous arrival. He peered around the inside of the cafe, until he spotted us.

"Bongiorno!" he shouted at us, but his enthusiasm suddenly wavered. He looked at us with some suspicion.

"Tedeschi?" he asked. "Deutsche?"

"No," I said, "Americani."

His boisterous energy returned at once. "Ah, Americani," he said, "va bene, va bene," and turning on his heel, he marched into the kitchen.

Almost immediately, the crash of pots and pans landing on the floor, accompanied by heavy expletives in Italian, came sailing out of the kitchen. Our hostess came out as well, a somewhat pained expression on her face.

"I'm sorry," she said. "You must forgive Giuseppe. He

has such a temper. All that noise just because he cannot find the lid of the stock pot. But he is such a wonderful cook. He can make the world's best 'gulyasch suppe', although he cannot speak a word of German."

Just then, the crashes inside the kitchen stopped, the kitchen door opened, and Giuseppe emerged grinning and holding a pot lid high over his head. "Vitoria!" he shouted, "Vitoria!" and he disappeared back into the kitchen. Our hostess smiled at the closing door, sighed, and began straightening up the tables, in apparent anticipation of lunch.

The first lunch customer, a ruddy-faced man in paint-stained overalls entered the cafe a few minutes later, stomping the snow from his feet. With him, on a leash, was a small black and white puppy, also coated with snow. The man dropped the leash, and the puppy, much as his master had done shook off the snow. That done, he came rushing over to our table, tail wagging, jumped up on Susan and settled down happily to chew on my shoelaces.

"Fritzschen," said the man. "Fritz, komm her." To all our surprise (I think even his own), Fritzschen sorrowfully abandoned my shoelaces and returned to his master as directed. The man reattached the leash, and looped the other end under the leg of his chair. I noticed that Fritzschen had a kink in his tail, as if he had perhaps broken it in a door.

"Er ist noch sehr jung. He is still very young," his owner said. "Too much happiness, perhaps." He reached down and rumpled the puppy's ears, noticing my gaze at Fritzchen's tail. "He broke it," he said. "He wagged it too hard."

Our hostess appeared out of the back where she had been wiping off a table. "Guten morgen, Herr Gerhardt, guten morgen Fritzchen." She bent down to tickle the puppy on his stomach. "We are not quite ready with the lunch."

"Guten morgen, Gisella," Gerhardt replied. "It doesn't matter, it's so nice and warm in here." He smiled and picked up last week's *Stern* magazine to read until lunch would be ready. "Meanwhile, am I allowed a beer while I wait?" he asked.

Gerdhart did not have to wait long. Within five or ten minutes the clock on the Grossmunster Cathedral began to chime the hour of twelve. The eleventh gong had barely struck when Giuseppe struggled out of the kitchen door carrying a large blackboard.

** MITTAGESSEN **

was written in bold letters across the top. And then:

Gulyasch Suppe Bratwurst mit Kartoffel - Salat Rindfleisch mit Mehretich Sosse - Leberkase mit Spiegel - Schnitzel mit Ei und Grune Bohnen

Across the bottom, in the same bold letters:

* HEUTE, RAVIOLI GIUSEPPE *

He stopped in front of our table, and set the board on the floor for us to see. "Lei mangia qui? What will you have?" he asked. "Buono, molto buono," he said pointing to the star billing for the Ravioli Giuseppe.

I tried to explain that we had to head back to our hotel for lunch, but Giuseppe either did not understand or did not want to. He scowled, sighed, then laughed and carried his signboard out through the heavy green drapes to prop it outside, by the front door.

A moment later, he came back inside holding his apron as a kind of umbrella over the heads of a haggard-looking woman dressed all in black, and a small, thin, sallow-skinned boy, perhaps eight or ten years old. They looked Jewish. The woman's coat was far too light for the weather and we could see her shivering from across the room, while she tried, by rubbing him, to warm up the boy. Gisella, emerging through the kitchen door, looked once around the cafe, then walked quickly to the woman. She looked some three inches taller than before.

"Komm," she said in German, in a tone I had not heard her speak before. "Take off those clothes. They are all wet. Come here to the stove, where it is warm. Giuseppe?" she snapped in Italian, "more coal. And bring some hot soup. Not ravioli. Soup!" Giuseppe scurried into the kitchen.

The woman, still shivering, stood close to the stove, with

78

the boy between her and the heat. Neither had said a word since they entered the cafe.

Finally, the woman screwed up her courage. "Is this the right place?" she whispered. Our hostess nodded.

"Of course," she said. "Do you think we do this with everyone?"

Giuseppe was coming out the kitchen door with the soup when the front door opened and a gust of cold air swept in between the blankets which Giuseppe had left slightly open when he went out with the board. Gisella leaped to the curtains, and with one hand held them shut. "Quick," she hissed, "into the kitchen." Putting his broad back between the boy and his mother and the front door, Giuseppe herded them into the kitchen. It is amazing, I thought to myself, how quickly fat men can move if they have to.

Meanwhile, on the outside of the door blanket curtains, an imperious voice was cursing and tearing at the blankets in its effort to get in. "Was fur scheisse ist dass, diese verdammt vorhange. What is this shit, these goddamn drapes," he shouted. Checking to make sure the boy and his mother were out of sight in the kitchen, Gisella loosened her grip on the blankets and a small paunchy man with a Hitler mustache strode into the cafe. There was a small gold swastika on his lapel. "Was fur scheisse soll dass sein?" he snarled. "What kind of shit is this?" he said again. He glared around the cafe at Gerhardt and his dog, and the man and finally, at us.

79

"Who are they?" he barked.

Gisella had returned to her gentle submissive self. She was again three inches shorter as she took the man's expensive woolen coat and hung it on the rack by the door.

"I'm so sorry to have upset you, Herr Geheimrat. I was trying to open the curtains for your arrival, and instead I seem to have kept them shut. I am so sorry, Herr Geheimrat. I know how hard you work for us on the City Council. You don't need more aggravation when you come to my cafe..."

Her speech seemed to have calmed him down somewhat, and he sat down heavily in a booth for six.

"Coffee," he barked. And then he looked around the café once again. "I asked you," he said to Gisella, "who are they?" He motioned in our direction.

She came over to him bearing a steaming coffee cup. "They are Americans," she said, "American tourists." She set the cup in front of him.

"Dass hab ich mir gedacht. That's what I thought." And I thought I heard him say under his breath, in German, "goddamn American Jews."

A few more customers began to drift in, a pretty young student from the University, a man with a small beard, playing mountain tunes on his harmonica, a group of workers from the construction site down the road, who tried by various antics to impress the girl. But the magic was gone from the place.

I called for our check, and Gisella came over to our table

without it. "I'm sorry," she said. "He is the vice chairman of the City Council, and an important member of the Nazi party...There will be no charge," she added. But, I protested, the fault was not hers. "Come back tomorrow," she said. "Tomorrow you can pay."

"All right," I said, "tomorrow we will pay."

As we got up to leave, I looked for the first time down at the *Zuricher Nachrichten* lying on the table. I could have sworn that the date, in small letters near the top, read 13 Marz 1938. I am quite nearsighted, and I was going to look closer, but Susan had already passed the *Geheimrat* Privy Councilor, sitting alone at his table dripping *gulyasch suppe* on his vest, and was passing through the green blankets on her way out the door. I hurried after her.

The lunch at the Shapirohof was excellent, as was dinner later on at the Mechanic's Guildhall restaurant across the river, in the elegant part of town. Well stuffed, like a Swiss goose, we headed back across the Limmat River to our home at the Shapirohof.

We awoke early the next morning. It had snowed again during the night, and the wet snow clung to the trees outside our windows. "Are you hungry?" Susan asked from under our featherbed.

"No," I said, "You?" After 34 years of marriage you tend to think the same thought at the same time.

"Well, let's go to the cafe," she said.

In ten minutes, we were dressed, and walking down the

street in front of the hotel toward the cafe. The snow was soft under foot, and our feet slipped a little as we walked down past the cross street below ours, and reached the avenue. We turned right, and continued to walk through the lightly falling snow, until we realized we had reached the end of the block. Susan looked at me.

"We must have walked by it," she said, although neither one of us believed it.

We walked back up the avenue. The cafe was not there. Where it had been, there was now a high concrete retaining wall, which held up what appeared to be a schoolyard above.

"We must have gone the wrong way," I said. "Maybe we should have turned left." We followed the avenue three blocks up the hill, then five blocks back down. The cafe was not there.

"Let's check the next avenue down the hill," Susan said, but we both knew we were fooling ourselves.

A bell sounded from up the avenue, and a tram filled with people on their way to work slid by, a large "6" on its side. "There's no point," I said. "This is the right avenue. There's the number 6 tram." Susan nodded. Nevertheless, we walked down to the next avenue down the hill. There was no tram, and no cafe.

Back up on the right avenue, we decided to walk one last time down the block where the cafe had been. As we came near the spot, a small black and white dog emerged from a narrow alley, glanced briefly at us, and went trotting down the hill. I was looking for the fourth or fifth time at the retaining wall where the cafe had been. Suddenly, Susan shouted something. At first I missed it.

"Look," she said, "Look! There's a crick in his tail. It's Fritz, it's Fritzchen! Come, Fritzchen, come here Fritz," she called.

The little dog stopped, looked back at us, wagged his crimped tail just once, then turned and continued trotting down the avenue.

"We've got to get him," Susan said, and she took off running down the avenue, slipping, sliding, running, with me a bit behind. The dog stayed some 50 meters ahead of us, then veered off into the next street on the right. Susan and I came puffing up to the corner, but Fritzchen was nowhere in sight, and there were no paw prints in the snow.

We walked up and down the street shouting for him. "Here Fritz, here, Fritzchen," but he did not appear. Someone opened a window in one of the houses which lined the street and shouted "Ruhe! Silence!" He had a right to be upset. It was only 7:00 in the morning. We gave up the search, and walked slowly back to the avenue, just as another number 6 tram was gliding by. On the front of the tram was an electric sign showing its route. It read "Zeitgasse".

"Zeitgasse", in English, is the "Street of Time".

ONKEL THEODOR

My great uncle, retired Ambassador Theodor von Hornbostel, died 50 years ago in Austria. During most of World War I, he had been a very young Consul General in St. Petersburg. He spoke 12 languages, including German, French, English, Russian, Greek, Polish, Mandarin, Norwegian, Hungarian, Spanish, Portuguese and Czech and told some astonishing stories.

One day in 1917 he had received a telegram from Vienna ordering him to close down the consulate, and take all of the important files to Moscow. The Russian Revolution was in full swing, and hyperinflation was rapidly destroying the value of any cash the consulate had. He was told to spend whatever he needed to get to Moscow, and bring the rest with him.

"So," he said, "I closed down the Consulate, burned most of the papers. I put the cash I still had in a cigar box, and went down to the train station, with the revolution going on all around my ears. I got to the station, and went up to the *guichet* to buy my ticket. The ticket agent looked at me as if I were crazy."

"Vot tickets?" he said. "Zher are no tickets, zher are no trains. This is a revolution, comrade. Zher are not trains." And he went back to reading his girlie magazine.

So, I walked out onto the street and around the station toward the railroad yard in the back. I was sure, young man that I was, that there had to be some way to get to Moscow, and I turned the corner at the back of the station. There, on the siding, sat the most beautiful locomotive I had ever seen. It was deep black, with a brass bell and a brass whistle which sparkled in the sun, and gleaming steel wheels. It was still steaming a little, and there in the cab sat the engineer with a gray cap, puffing on his pipe.

So I went up to him. "Excuse me," I said, "could you please tell me who is the owner of this beautiful locomotive?"

The engineer looked down at me, and laughed. "It's my locomotive, comrade," he said. "It's a Revolution! It's the people's locomotive...it's my locomotive," he said again.

"Good." I said. "I'll buy it from you. How much do you want for it?"

He looked at me suspiciously. "It's not for sale," he said.

"Oh, come on," I said. "I'll pay cash. Name your price."

He looked down at me with a crafty look in his eye. "One million rubles," he said grandly.

"Done!" I said. "Now, how much will you charge to drive me to Moscow in it?"

The engineer took his time to reply. "Another million rubles," he said, as if speaking with a complete lunatic.

"Good," I said. We have a...what do you say...a deal." And I opened my cigar box and counted out two million rubles. They must have been worth perhaps 50 dollars. I thought he was going to faint on the spot.

"You'll have to shovel the coal," he croaked.

And so I traveled to Moscow, through the middle of the Russian Revolution, in my own locomotive, shoveling the coal. He turned out to be a nice man, my engineer. His name was Boris. When we got to Moscow, I gave the locomotive back to him...I didn't need a locomotive in Moscow.

*****

Onkel Theodor remained in the Austrian foreign service, and by 1937, he had become General Secretary, the highest ranking non-political post.

"I was also the highest ranking official in the Austrian Government to oppose the Anschluss," he said, "you know, the annexation of Austria by Germany. But in March of 1938, it happened nonetheless. I hated the Nazis — the only thing I wanted from them was to be the first one to be arrested after the Anschluss. The first to be arrested was the head of the Communist party, Kurt Stempel. I was sadly only the second one to be arrested."

"I was put on a cattle car with a bunch of common criminals, and shipped to the concentration camp at Dachau. The Nazis divided most of the camps into two parts: one for common criminals and the other for Jews. Political prisoners who weren't Jewish, which was my case, were put in with the common criminals. We had, I would say, maybe a 50/50 chance of survival. The Jews, of course, had no chance at all."

"I had never been in a prison before, and so had no idea what I should do to survive. But one day, as I was walking in the prison yard in front of the barracks, a prisoner whom I had never seen before pulled me aside. He was a small, wiry fellow, with darting eyes."

"Hey," he said. "you're new here, aren't you?" I nodded. "And you're a political prisoner, right?" I nodded again. "And you speak French."

"How do you know?" I asked.

"You were a diplomat," he said. "Diplomats speak French."

"How did you know I was a diplomat?" I asked him.

"Never mind," he said. "I know, and I am going to make you an offer you can't refuse. I am a professional thief, but I haven't been too lucky. It seems as if every time I steal something, they catch me. So I have come to know prisons and prison camps very well, in fact much better than I would like. My offer is this, you teach me French, and I will teach you how to survive here. I'll keep you alive."

"But why do you want to learn French?" I asked him.

"I told you," he said. "You didn't listen. I am tired of being a thief. Besides, I'm not good at it. If the goddamn Nazis ever get burned, and if the war ever ends, I want to open a little restaurant in Paris - a little brasserie. I love Paris...I want to spend the rest of my life there!"

"Have you been there often?" I asked him.

"I've never been there," he said, "but I know I'm going to love it."

"So, did you accept his offer?" I asked Onkel Theodor. He laughed.

"You see me here, don't you? You wouldn't if it weren't for him. The prisoners had to line up for inspection out in the yard every morning at 5:30," he continued. "We were divided into so-called 'platoons' and they would give us our work assignments for the day, sometimes inside the camp, sometimes working somewhere outside. One morning, maybe 3 months after I arrived at Dachau, I was awaiting my work assignment for the day when my friend the thief appeared next to me."

"Getzik," he hissed.

"That's not French," I said.

"This is no joke," he whispered. "Get sick! Now!" And he was gone.

I collapsed right there onto the ground clutching my stomach and screaming. Several of my fellow prisoners carried me back to the barracks and lay me down on my cot. I continued to scream until one of the guards threatened to blow my brains out if I didn't shut up. I was still lying there whimpering later in the morning when I heard several rounds of machine gun fire from just outside the camp.

My platoon never came back to the camp that night. The thief and I were the only members of the platoon who survived. I never found out why the others were slaughtered, nor how he knew.

Sometime in 1942, I was transferred from Dachau to the camp at Buchenwald. My friend, the thief, remained behind in Dachau, and it would be years before I saw him again. By this time, I could take care of myself pretty well, and his French was almost fluent.

I did not remain long in Buchenwald. I had been there less than a year when I was summoned to the office of the Camp Kommandant. "Heil Hitler," I said.

"And you speak Russian as well?"

My friend, the thief had taught me long ago never to volunteer any information about anything, but something told me that this time, I should respond truthfully.

"Yes."

He reached for his leather club and brought it full force across my neck. "Yes, what, you pig?"

"Yes, your excellency."

"Alright. Now get out. And thank the Führer. You are a very lucky man."

Two days later, I was loaded into a truck with several other prisoners. We drove for two days with no food, stopping only once to wait out an Allied air raid. In the end, I was ordered out of the truck in the suburbs of Landsberg and the workers at the arms factory there were either Russian prisoners of war or Poles. The German plant manager had perished in an explosion a few weeks before, and I was to be the new manager of the plant. A small platoon of SS kept the prisoners, including me, under control.

Apparently, the Allies didn't know of the existence of the plant. In any case, they never bombed us, and I remained in charge of the plant until the Eastern front rolled through in the winter of 1944. The other prisoners and I managed to arrange very successful periodic "accidents" which exploded most of what we produced. Throughout all of 1944, no more than one or two trainloads of materiel left the plant.

When the Russian army finally arrived, I was once again arrested and thrown in the cellar of a farmhouse that served as their field headquarters. The Russian Kommandant was sure I had to be a Nazi collaborator, or a spy. Worse yet, he was sure I knew what had happened to Stempel. For some reason, the Russians were extremely interested in him. I think they thought that after his arrest in Vienna at the time of the Anschluss, he had become a double agent for the Nazis. The Nazis had sent him to Buchenwald, but from there he had disappeared. Since I, too, had been in Buchenwald, and had also gotten out, the Russians were certain that I had to know where he was. The only problem was that he had disappeared from the camp in 1942.

I carefully explained this to the Russian Kommandant, but he simply refused to believe me.

"You're a lying Nazi," he shouted. "Throw him back in the cellar!"

Every day they dragged me back upstairs to be questioned. Sometimes I was beaten, sometimes not. Every time I would tell the Kommandant the same thing...what else could I tell him? It was the truth.

Gradually, after a few months, the beatings stopped. I was still questioned daily, but we also talked a little about our families, and about what we would do when the war was over. In fact, it was already over, but no one had informed me. The Kommandant didn't tell me, but he wasn't a bad man.

And then, one day, I was taken upstairs and brought before the Kommandant again - but something was different. He was sitting at his desk, plainly drunk, a bottle of cheap Polish vodka on the desk in front of him. There was also a telegram on the desk. On the arm of his chair, draping both an arm and an ankle over him, was...what do you call them...a prostitute, a Polish prostitute.

"Alright, Hornbostel," he said. "You might as well tell me the truth." He picked up the telegram. "I have been ordered to withdraw, and to bring no prisoners. I'm afraid we shall have to shoot you. So you might as well tell me the truth before you go." He looked very sad.

I told him again that Stempel was no longer in Buchenwald when I arrived there.

The Kommandant looked at me sadly for several seconds before he beckoned to the soldier who had brought me up from the cellar.

"Alright, Mikaelovitch," he said to the guard, "take him out and shoot him." He poured himself a large drink of vodka. "Do you want one, honey lamb?" he said to the prostitute.

She looked at him, and moved her ankle up and down his thigh, and then into his crotch. "Oh, big boy," she said, "why don't you let the old man go?"

The Kommandant looked at her hazily. She turned over the telegram. "It doesn't say you have to shoot him," she said. "It just says you should bring no prisoners." She leaned down and kissed his forehead, then nestled her head down onto his epaulets, close to this ear. "He can't do any harm," she whispered. "Let the old man go."

The Kommandant's eyes picked up a glimmer of a smile. "Will that make you happy, my little mouse?"

She nodded.

"Alright," he said to me. "Get out of here. Now!"

It took me more than a week to get back from Russian field headquarters to the plant. Though the war was over, there were Russian roadblocks everywhere, and I preferred to make my way through the woods and fields. I had planned to go back to Landsberg to pick up some clothes and other supplies, and then make my way back to Austria. But when I arrived in Landsberg, I was arrested once again and brought before the new Kommandant of the local occupation forces.

To my relief, this Kommandant, Colonel Nicolai Menchikov, had never heard of Stempel. He did, however, desperately need someone who spoke Russian, Polish and German to assist the occupation forces to administer the town. And so, I was appointed mayor of Landsberg. Since the war was over, I repeatedly asked Colonel Menchikov to let me go home, but he was adamant.

"I need you here," he said. "Later, you can go home. "When we are a little better organized," he would say. But I wondered if that level of organization would ever happen.

One day, as I was working in my office in the basement of the Town Hall, I received a visit from a young man from the International Red Cross. Early in the war, the Germans had sent a large number of suitably Arian children to the Austrian alps - several stayed quite near there - to protect them against Allied bomb attacks. Now that the war was over, the Red Cross was trying to bring these children back to their families in Germany.

The young man explained that the Red Cross had just delivered a busload of youngsters back to Landsberg, but that now the Occupation forces had seized the bus and were refusing to return it. The Red Cross was desperate, since it had only the one bus with which to bring the children home. The young man begged me to intercede with Colonel Menchikov. I told him I would try.

The Colonel was, however, no help.

"Hornbostel," he said, "You are too soft-hearted. You know our biggest problem is transportation, and we need that bus for all sorts of purposes. If the Red Cross will get me a good truck to replace it, they can have their damn bus. Otherwise, no dice..." I had to tell the young man from the Red Cross that things did not look good.

But a month or so later, I had an idea. We had, in Landsberg, a prisoner of war hospital. Most of the prisoners were young Austrians who had been thrown into the Eastern Front late in 1944 in a desperate, unsuccessful German effort to stop the Russian advance. I knew them fairly well as an Austrian diplomat, and thought it my duty to do what I could to make them as comfortable as possible. Colonel Menchikov, however, was constantly complaining that, notwithstanding the general shortage of food, the prisoners always seemed to be very well fed.

"My soldiers go hungry," he grumbled, "while your goddamn useless Austrians are eating pork chops and potatoes." If he thought he could get away with it, he would probably have shot them all.

One morning, I walked over to Occupation Headquarters and without knocking, walked straight into the Colonel's office. "Colonel, I have a great idea," I said. "We can get rid of those Austrian leeches. Now that we have a bus, we can load those bloody parasites on the bus and dump them back in Austria. It shouldn't take more than a couple of trips. I'll even drive the bus, if you like..."

Colonel Menchikov looked at me suspiciously. "How do I know you'll bring the bus back?" he said.

"It's obvious," I said. "The bus holds 64 passengers. There are 122 prisoners. We'll have to make two trips. I have to come back or we won't get rid of them all. And I couldn't possibly take just some of them."

"I'll think about it," he said.

The next morning, he gave me the keys to the bus, together with a *laissez-passe* directing all Occupation Forces to allow us free passage through the occupied territories.

"Hurry back!" he said gruffly.

"I will," I said.

I drove the bus to the hospital, and we squeezed in all 122 Austrian prisoners. For the next 48 hours, I drove without stopping, except to buy, beg or steal gas, until we arrived in Austria, and I turned myself and my charges over to the head of the American Occupation Forces in Salzburg.

The bus was delivered back to the Red Cross, with an

admonition not to be so trusting of the Russians in the future.

*****

"Mein Gott, it's so late! I have to go," Onkel Theodor said. We'll talk some more next time."

"Onkel Theodor," I asked him. "Just one last question. What happened to the thief who saved you?"

"Oh, yes," he said. "I think it was 1947 when I received a beautiful engraved invitation in the mail to the inauguration of 'Brasserie André' in Saint-Germain-des-Prés in Paris. I went, of course. It was a wonderful party, I think the best I have ever been to. The food was delicious, and my friend was so happy. He was the perfect restauranteur."

"So, gute nacht, my dear. We'll talk some more soon. À bientôt!"

But sadly, we never talked again. Onkel Theodor passed on later that year.

AMAZONAS

The night boat to Santarém left Manaus, in true Brazilian fashion, about an hour late. She was one of the last to leave, and by the time her bowsprit nosed out into the black waters of the Rio Negro, only a few beggars, the fried plantain vendor, a policeman and two or three whores were left on the shore. The whores were not pretty. They were not surprised to be left behind.

Just before the gangplank came in, a thin old gentleman strode aboard, wearing a great wide-brimmed straw hat, a ragged white suit jacket, and well-patched trousers. As if he had been waiting for the old man, the Captain rang three bells in the engine room, the engines shuddered into reverse, and the steamer slid away from the shore.

We cruised for about ten minutes down the river before the bells rang again, the engines slowed, and the old wooden ship nosed her way in toward the riverbank at what looked like a large mining complex. Heavy trucks were being loaded onto ferry boats, while other trucks hurried them along from behind, the bright shafts of their headlights cutting through the darkness. The captain slowly brought the bow of the N.M. Moreira da Silva III up to one of the ferry boats that were moored to an aging pier.

A voice came from the shore. "Hey, you can't land here," it shouted in rough Portuguese. "It's prohibited."

"But we're landing the Captain ashore," the mate of our ship shouted from the upper deck. "It's very important."

"I don't care who he is, you can't land him on the ferry boat."

More shouting back and forth. The man on the shore appeared to be some kind of a local authority, perhaps a policeman. In the shadow of the bowsprit, the old man with the hat lowered himself onto the deck of the ferry boat, and with a firm step, walked past the guard and into the night.

"Alright," shouted the mate. "We're leaving. A fond embrace to you, my friend. And go screw yourself!"

An oath came back from the shore.

"Bullshit," said Paulo. "The old man is no more the Captain than I am..." Paulo is my oldest friend in Brazil. He is from Rio de Janeiro and is nobody's fool. Paulo was right. A day or two later, we asked the real Captain, Sr. Gato, about the old man.

"Hell no," he said. "That's Father Time. He lives on the river near the gringo mining company. He rides with us now and then, and we like to give him door to door service. Two hundred and fifty feet of river steamer giving door to door service.

"You charge him a lot for that?" I asked.

"We don't charge him at all" The captain said.

It turned out that Sr. Moreira da Silva himself was on board, sleeping with his gorgeous young wife and six month old son in the forward cabin that had a plaque over the door that said "owner". For the owner of what, based on its name, must have been his third steamer, Sr. Moreira da Silva was not an impressive looking man.

He stood maybe 5'6" in his stocking feet, with mousy hair and muddy eyes, and a small, wispy mustache. He spoke softly, if at all, and mostly walked around the boat carrying his infant son, and tickling his stomach. Not an impressive looking man, but gentle, and his employees, while treating him with appropriate deference, did not fear him. Antonio, the master of the engine room, said that "Sr. João" also owned a supermarket in Manaus, and it was not hard to imagine him behind the cash register, or counting bananas or pineapples in his store.

But what a wife! Great God in heaven! A tall, brown-skinned girl with jet black hair, flashing black eyes, brilliant white teeth, and a body that would knock you flat just to look at her. Perhaps there was more to Sr. João than met the eye, or at least her eyes, like for instance, the bank account that had bought the Moreira da Silva III, and the supermarket, and the nice clothes on his gorgeous young wife.

What a woman, only the famed Jorge Amado could have done her justice. She reminded me of Teresa Batista in her younger years, before she tired of the wars, or maybe Gabriela, Clove and Cinnamon. But the boys kept their eyes, and their hands off her. Regular paying jobs aren't easy to come by in the Amazon.

There were two classes of service on the Moreira da Silva III.

In first class you had the right to hang your hammock on the upper deck. In tourist, you slept downstairs with the chickens and the pigs and the other cargo. First class was $11.00 for the three day trip to Santarém, including food, tourist class was $9.00. We decided to splurge. We hung our hammocks on the upper deck. The cool breeze off the world's greatest river made them swing gently in the darkness. By late in the night only a few hundred kilometers from the equator, I would wish I had a blanket.

The fellow in the next hammock over was on his way to see his dying father in Santarém. Paulo dubbed him the "Cowboy". Skinny, long dirty hair, worn jeans, cowboy boots, lousy teeth and nothing on his mind but sex. For that, it wasn't such a great trip. Even the Cowboy wasn't about to mess with Moreira's wife, and beyond her, the pickings were slim. But Cowboy was undaunted.

As we were hanging our hammocks, Tania, the cleaning girl and kitchen helper, walked by in a tight pair of Bermuda shorts. "Look at the ass on her," he hissed. Cowboy was up out of his hammock and following her down the stairs to the lower deck. He gave me a broad wink and a dig in the ribs as he hurried past.

The Moreira da Silva III leapfrogged her way down the Amazon, stopping now to drop a passenger at a grass shack along the great river, or to pick up another, or to buy a *tucunaré*, a giant river fish, from an Indian boy who came paddling out to greet us, squatting in the front of his dugout canoe. Around 10 o'clock Saturday night we passed a great conglomeration of small boats on the shore, and the music of the *"forro"* came booming out over the water. The word *"forro"* comes from the English "for all," and on shore, you could see them all dancing like ants on a flattened anthill. Antonio was up on deck, taking a break from the engine room.

"That's where I should be," Antonio sighed. "That's where the life is." He spat over the side and took a long drag on his beer.

Moreira walked by, trying to rock his son to sleep. "That is the place to be, eh, Sr. João? How about a little run ashore?" Antonio insisted. But either Sr. João hadn't heard, or he didn't fancy the idea. He smiled his mousy smile, and padded back to his cabin. He didn't need the *Forro*. He had what he needed, right on board.

At 4:00 in the morning, we reached Obidos. Paulo woke

me to see it. It seemed to be a beautiful old town, with churches and houses that looked as if they dated from colonial times, built with money from the rubber trade. The town had died when King Rubber died, a century before. You couldn't see much in the dark.

Apparently no one needed to go ashore in Obidos. We loaded on three crates of live chickens, some lemons, and moved on.

*****

Breakfast on the Moreira was adequate, but certainly nothing more. There were two great thermos bottles on the table, one with hot, sweet coffee, one with hot milk. A great bag of hard, flat salt crackers lay next to the coffee together with a cup of margarine. You helped yourself.

But lunch was something else. Promptly at 10:30 a.m. Tania came through the upper deck.

"Lunch," she whispered to me so the other passengers wouldn't hear. "Hustle, or you won't get a place."

She was right. By the time I got to the table, it was full of men, and Tania was putting great steaming bowls down on the middle of the table, one with spaghetti, one with rice, one with beans, another with gristly, but tasty, stewed meat and, of course, one with *farofa*, the universal Brazilian dish made of ground, toasted manioc. I found a place near the end of the table, and sat down. Paulo squeezed in opposite. Tania brought another great plate of meat and set it in front of us. No one spoke.

The food moved as quickly as possible from platter to plate, and finally into the hungry mouths of the passengers and crew. This was serious business, not a time to talk. Only Paulo and I spoke. By the time we were half finished with our meal, the others had gotten up and left, and Jeronimo, the cook, was asking us politely how soon we would be finished so that he could serve the second shift.

We reached Parintins by early afternoon, and Paulo and I walked around the town while the crew unloaded some 500 cases of *guaraná* soda onto the shore. Antonio lifted the cover and four of the crew dropped into the hold. One by one they reappeared, bodies glistening with sweat, their arms thrust high with two cases of soda each time, as if reaching for God to pull them up from hell. But it was Antonio, not God, who took the cases from their hands with no apparent effort at all, and slid them down two planks to the shore. The Moreira waited a good time after the soda was all ashore until Sr. João appeared, driving a well-used red Volkswagen bug. The bug came aboard on the same planks on which the soda had left. Then, with a great ringing of bells, Antonio started up the engines, and the Moreira slid back out into the river.

By nightfall, Cowboy hadn't advanced very far with Tania, and was reduced to regaling us with his sexual exploits on his last trip to Belém. A young wiry member of the crew they called "Enraba Onça" joined us with a few stories of his own. I listened in the dark, my hammock swaying in the breeze, until I fell asleep. I woke up with the Moreira pitching fairly hard in the river, my hammock swinging wildly, and a tropical rainstorm pounding down on the tin roof of the upper deck. There was someone holding onto my hammock in the darkness.

"Come," said Tania. "You'll freeze out here."

She took my hand and led me forward through the sheeting rain to her tiny cabin just behind the bridge.

"Take that off," she said, pointing to my dripping shirt. "You'll be warm here." She lit a candle and I took off my shirt and handed it to her. "Those, too," she said, pointing to my shorts.

I climbed into the lower bunk and took them off. A moment later, Tania climbed into the bunk with me while the tropical storm raged. "I want more," she said. "Now we'll get warm," she said, sliding next to me.

*****

The next morning dawned bright and clear, and by the time I slipped out of Tania's cabin and downstairs to wash in the sinks next to the mess cabin, the crew was up and working.

Sr. Oswaldo was the Moreira's second everything, second mate, second helmsman, second engineer, second cook. He had two wives, one in Santarém and the other in Manaus, but neither of them was "second wife," he said. His "official" wife, the one he was married to "on paper", had given him four kids, all grown now. His daughter was a lawyer with a leading bank, another was a doctor, a third was an engineer, and the fourth had a small construction firm. "I've got no worries," Oswaldo had said to me, his great belly hanging over the wheel as he steered with his bare feet. "I'm a gentle tide."

He chuckled. "I'll make more money on this trip than Sr. João makes with his whole damn boat." He didn't explain how, and I didn't ask.

Now Sr. Oswaldo was sitting at the breakfast table, chomping salt biscuits with margarine and drinking his coffee with milk. He grunted in reply to my greeting.

"Where you fellows going to sleep in Santarém?"

"I don't know," I said. "You have a suggestion?"

"Why don't you stay on the boat," he said.

"What about Sr. João? We don't head back to Manaus until Thursday." Sr. Oswaldo helped himself to another fistful of salt biscuits.

"Don't worry about Sr. João," he said. "He'll be delighted."

*****

The city of Santarém sprawls along the south bank of the Rio Tapajós, just before it pours into the main stream of the muddy Amazon. The waters of the Tapajós are blue-green and clear, and there are white sand beaches along the shore at Maracanã, and

Maria da Graça, and at Altar do Chão. Above Santarém, the Tapajós is wider than the mighty Amazon itself, a huge calm blue-green sea stretching to the horizon and beyond.

By the time the Moreira nosed into the breakwater a little after 6:00 a.m., the market along the shore was already swarming with vendors, customers, hawkers, gawkers, con men, schoolgirls, old men, young men, drifters, sailors, fishermen, housewives - in short, the whole town was out in the market, taking advantage of the morning cool before the sun rose any higher in the enormous Amazon sky. And smiling there above it all, on the billboard above the square, was the huge jowly face of a very fat man, looking as if he were about to belch and glad of it, with a smile that seemed to say "I've got mine. Pretty soon I'll have yours."

"Ronaldo for Mayor," said the billboard, and the great jowls belched and smiled.

For the rest of our stay, Ronaldo was like the river itself, a constant presence. His smile gazed benignly down from dozens of billboards all over the town. Every fence and wall bore his name. On every lamp post, a smaller poster bore his visage and announced him. Ronaldo had truly blanketed the town.

There was, of course, an opposition. Ronan Liberal was fat as well, but the jowls were less repulsive, perhaps because his campaign avoided the giant billboards, using more discreet, smaller photos instead. Even so, there was plenty of him, and the banners across Main Street announced his candidacy in garish pink. Although the election was still three months away, a few of

Ronaldo's posters had already been spattered with blobs of ink, thrown from a speeding car by a team of lads, presumably Ronan supporters, the week before.

The sullied posters looked a bit as if Ronaldo had belched up a few of yesterday's black beans. But the smile remained in place. "They're old friends, actually," Sr. Oswaldo told us. "And they're both rich as Croesus. Ronaldo is a federal representative, you know."

He waved at a large house next to the hotel on the shore. "That's his mama's place, where he grew up. Now you know he's not coming home from Brasilia just to live with mama." He grinned.

"Will he beat Ronan?"

Oswaldo shrugged. "Who cares," he said.

The Santarém Globo newspaper was somewhat kinder. As a successful federal representative, it said, Ronaldo seemed to have the advantage. Of course, it pointed out, Ronan was a former mayor, appointed by the government in the days before democracy had returned to Brazil, and hadn't led an excellent administration. "But that can be blamed on poor advisors," the newspaper story added apologetically.

There were boats of every size tied up to the great concrete bulkhead which keeps the Tapajós river from inundating the town. All but the smallest dugout canoes were painted white, and the river steamers had signs hanging from the railings near the bridge:

"Leaves today for Belém with intermittent stops."

"Leaves Wednesday 6:00 p.m. for Manaus. Stopping at Obidos, Parintins and on demand."

"Leaves 7:00 p.m. TODAY for Monte Alegre."

The smaller boats had no signs: the customers already knew exactly where the boats went, and had no need for instructions. We passed another large steamer:

"Leaves at noon for Itaituba, arrives tomorrow at 2:00."

Paulo nudged me. Swinging in a dirty hammock on the afterdeck was a scruffy looking individual with a red beard and a Colt 45 strapped to his leg. "Gold mining country," Paulo said. He stared at the boat.

"Next trip," I said.

"OK," he agreed.

On the land side of the bulkhead, the street vendors were selling every conceivable type of fruit: pineapple, oranges, tangerines, lemons, *fruta do conde*, *jabuticaba*, papayas, coconuts, mangoes, star fruit, a bunch of others I had never heard of, and what seemed to be an absolutely endless variety of bananas: red, green, yellow, orange, brown, huge plantains, tiny banana prata, and all, as the Brazilians say, at "*preço de banana*," that is to say, practically free.

We bought a dozen banana prata for the equivalent of 9 cents and ate them as we walked along the quay. Here and there among the stalls were tiny restaurants, a few boards made into a rough table and shaded by a burlap sack. Each had a small brazier with fresh whole fish grilling over the coals. A withered old lady looked up at us.

"What kind of fish do you have, grandma?" Paulo asked her.

"*Tucunaré*," she said. "Caught this morning."

"How much?"

"25 cents each," she said. "With fried *farinha de mandioca*."

It was expensive by Amazonas standards, but we were tourists, and the old woman needed the customers. We sat down. The *tucunaré* was delicious, fresh, moist and sweet, tinged with the smoky flavor of the charcoal. Her grandson ran across the way and bought us a frosty cold beer.

There isn't anything much better than eating grilled *tucunaré* on the banks of the Tapajós river and washing it down with ice cold Brahma beer.

"Lovely fish, grandma."

The old lady beamed.

We walked out past the edge of the town to where the boats and the vendors thinned down and finally ended altogether, then turned inland until we reached the Hotel Tropical, built 20 years before by a Brazilian airline, and parked like a beached ocean liner on the dunes above the Tapajós.

Outside, one middle-aged tourist lady lay stretched in the sun by the side of the pool. A uniformed desk clerk, wearing the only necktie I had seen in Santarém, eyed us suspiciously. Paulo stared him coldly in the eye. His mustache bristled.

"Dr. Freitas de Guimarães Canto e Melo, por favor."

"There's no one registered here by that name. I know the guest list."

"How do you know? You haven't even checked. How many guests do you have registered?"

"Seven."

"Well, when Dr. Freitas arrives, tell him that Paulo Rocha Sarney was looking for him."

The effect was electric. At the mention of "Sarney," the name of the president of Brazil, the clerk turned to jelly. His black necktie seemed to wilt on the vine, his voice quivered.

"But Dr. Paulo, isn't there something I can do for you sir, a cafézinho perhaps, a nice chilled glass of mineral water?"

Paulo scowled. "I'd like to use the bathroom," he said. The clerk hurried around the counter.

"Yes, of course, Dr. Paulo. Right this way. A pleasure, Dr. Paulo."

Paulo looked over to me and grinned. "Come on," he said in English. "We'll have a wash and a nice clean crap in a toilet that doesn't stink."

We rented a VW bug from the car rental on the lower level of the hotel, and headed out of town toward Altar do Chão. Paulo drove. Ever since I first met him, in the middle of a tremendous tropical storm in Rio de Janeiro in January of 1965, Paulo's first love was cars. Any kind of cars, from Formula I to Volkswagens.

Now he successfully dodged huge potholes, chickens, streams, children, garbage, and an alligator. Our bug almost disappeared in some of the ruts in the road, but it never lost traction.

The trip to Altar do Chão is only 35 kilometers from Santarém, but it is enough to give a bit of a feel of the Amazon jungle. Most of the giant trees had been cut and hauled away, but here and there, sometimes in the middle of the road, a giant *castanheira* cashew tree reached its branches 100 feet or more into the pale tropical sky.

There were a few houses along the road, made of dry palm fronds woven together into perfect beige mosaics, next to bits of cultivated ground where farmers eked out their existence planting manioc. We stopped and gave a ride to two little boys coming home from school.

"Oh yes," they said, "there were leopards in this jungle, and monkeys, and sloths, and armadillos, and parrots, and alligators..."

"And elephants," Paulo said. The older of the boys nodded agreement.

"Yes, but they only come out at night," he added.

Altar do Chão means "Altar of Earth". It deserves the name. There is a "mountain" perhaps 200 feet high (in the Amazon, that's a mountain), and the waters of the Tapajós curl around its feet in a soft embrace before they spread into a series of blue-green lagoons, framed in clean white sand and set against the deep green of the jungle. A sandbar stretches almost across the lagoon, and the white sand is dotted with trees.

Paulo parked the car in the shade of a small tree, and we both plunged into the water. The water was soft and clear, and I stayed down near the bottom until my lungs no longer held, watching the sun making prisms on the surface. I headed up, took a great gulp of the moist, warm air, and plunged down again. When I came to the surface again, Paulo was sitting in the shallow water, a foolish smile on his face.

"It's not salty," he said happily. "It's not salty at all." He bent over and took a small sip of the river. "Try it," he said. "It's really sweet water."

He had never swum in freshwater before. You won't find that in Rio de Janeiro.

We walked down the beach a short distance to the village. Next to the church, a sign announced "Mingote's Restaurant". Sr. Mingote himself sat at one of his tables in the shade of a spreading mango tree. He was the first human being we had seen in Altar do Chão. Paulo sat down next to the old man.

"Sr. Mingote?" he asked.

The old man nodded.

"Is the beer cold?"

"Po*is claro*, of course," Sr. Mingote replied.

"And the fish fresh?"

"Caught 'em this morning."

"So let's eat them now."

Mingote got reluctantly to his feet, and wandered off

toward the kitchen. But the beer came quickly and was icy cold. And the fish were as fresh as promised, and fried to a turn. After lunch, we left the car keys with Sr. Mingote and swam across the lagoon to the sandbar with the trees.

The sand was hard near the water's edge, and we walked easily the mile or so to the rocky rubble that was the "altar". It had a large cross on its flattened top, and a foot trail wound up the side. In 15 minutes we were at the top. The cross stood a good 20 feet high and was made of two old electric poles. A couple of insulators remained stuck, like warts, on the cross piece. The view was superb. In every direction, the waters of the Tapajós sparkled in the sun, broken here and there by the white sand. Just below, the green of the jungle swept up to the beaches. Beyond the sandbar, a church steeple poked into the horizon.

"Sr. Mingote," Paulo shouted, waving at the restaurant now a kilometer away. "Sr. Mingote, you are the sacristan, the keeper of the altar. This is truly a place of God." If Sr. Mingote replied, we didn't hear him. It was dark by the time we left Altar do Chão and drove back through the jungle to Santarém.

Paulo parked the bug across the quay from the Moreira da Silva III and stepped outside. "Look," he said.

Perched on the electric wires that stretched from post to post along the shore, were literally thousands of swallows squeezed in line next to one another and filling the wires with countless bumps.

"I'm glad we are not sleeping up there," said Paulo.

"There's no vacancy."

For the remainder of our stay in Santarém, the swallows returned nightly, sweeping in over the Moreira in great swirling clouds of tiny black birds that, by some miracle, managed to avoid collision. They arrived always at the same time, just before nightfall. Their preferred location was between the Moreira and the Banco Amazonas de Santarém bank. Stragglers had to content themselves with sleeping in front of Julio's bar down the block, in front of the Moreira. Everything was always packed.

The crew had mostly gone ashore by the time we arrived and Tania had gone to her mother's house. Paulo and I showered and changed on board, and headed "downtown." It was amazing. Where thousands of people had swarmed the streets like ants at 6:00 in the morning, now, twelve hours later, there was no one. Not a vendor, not a straggler, not a drunk. It was as empty now as it had been full and Julio's Bar provided the only beacon of light, proof that the city still lived. We sat under the streetlight at one of the tables outside. Julio wandered over.

"Evening, gentlemen," he said. "*Caipirinhas*, will it be?"

I nodded.

Julio went back to the bar to cut up the green lemons for our *caipirinhas*, and we watched the swallows making their final adjustments for the night. Sr. Julio came back from the bar.

"Do you like them sweet?" he asked.

"Not too sweet."

"OK," he said.

I watched him return to the bar and carefully measure a tablespoon of sugar into the glass with chunks of green lemon in it. Then he took a wooden pestle and crushed them together.

Sr. Julio looked out across the tables to where we sat. "Ice?" he called.

"Lots," Paulo said.

We watched as Sr. Julio cracked the ice, then took a large jug covered in woven rattan, and filled each glass with cachaça Brazil's sugar-based equivalent of Kentucky white lightning. He brought the two *caipirinhas* over on a tray, and set them on the table.

"Are the birds always here?" Paulo asked.

Julio looked up. "No," he said.

"Come fall they head north, back to your country, I guess," he said, nodding at me.

"They're gone by December, and return in May. And they always sleep just there, every year since they put the electric lines in. Every year they're back. I don't know how they find it, they cross several thousand kilometers of 'civilization' and a couple of thousand more of jungle, and then, one day in May, here they are, in front of my bar in Santarém, as if they'd never left. At least they've got good taste." He laughed and the gold cap on his front tooth glinted in the light of the street light.

"What are you gentlemen going to eat? The fish stew is good."

"What else is there?"

Julio's brow face broke back into a grin. "Like I told you, the fish stew is good."

"I'll have the fish stew," said Paulo.

"Now, there's a sensible lad," said Julio.

He turned to me. "What would you like, sir?"

The fish stew was delicious, great chunks of Pacu fish in a stew of tomatoes, onions, yellow squash, and coconut milk. It came with a mountain of white rice, a bowl of toasted manioc and a small dish of pepper sauce. There was plenty of food. I had almost finished my first plateful of the stew when Newton appeared. By his size, he could not have been more than six or seven (I later learned he was nine), but the street-wise look in his eye belonged to a kid of fifteen.

"Hi," he said. "I'm Newton," and without more ado he slid into an empty chair at the table. "Are you going to eat all of that?"

I looked over. Newton was wearing nothing but a pair of ragged shorts. Except for his brown, dust coated feet, he looked clean. He did not look undernourished. Plainly he was good at what he was now doing.

"I don't know yet," I said. "Are you very hungry?"

He nodded very solemnly, and put on a set of almost weepy Walt Kuhn eyes. Julio came hustling over.

"Out of here, you little thief," he shouted, swatting at the kid with his apron.

"Wait. Let him be," said Paulo. "We invited him to

dinner." Sr. Julio looked doubtful.

"You're sure he is not bothering you?"

"No, he's fine."

"Could you please bring another plate and a spoon?" Julio was muttering to himself as he walked away, but he returned with the plate and spoon as requested.

"D'you think I could have a plastic bag instead?" said Newton.

I looked at him. "Why do you want a plastic bag?" I said.

"So I can take it home to my brothers and sisters," said Newton.

"Bullshit," said Julio. "He'll take it and sell it to the vendors who sleep down by the water. Or maybe he'll sell it to one of the other urchins."

"No plastic bag," I said. "You sit and eat right here."

I never learned the truth of it, but this much was true: there wasn't a bite of food we offered Newton over the next couple of days that he did not share with his chums, who also shared with the streets of Santarém. As soon as Julio retreated to his bar, two of those chums appeared out of the shadows.

The older of the two was a beautiful brown-skinned boy of perhaps 10, with sad, almond shaped eyes. Tagging along with him, with slightly buck teeth and ears sticking straight out from the side of his head, was a little fellow who looked like somebody's little brown bunny. These guys were a good deal shyer than Newton, and stood watching us a little ways from the table.

"Come on over," said Newton to them. "This is Roberto," he said, pointing to the taller one.

"And this is Lindomar. They're my friends." The boys came over.

"You guys want something to eat?" asked Newton.

Lindomar nodded. Then he came over and took my spoon and rapidly tucked into Newton's plate.

"Don't you want to eat?" I asked Roberto.

"No," he said. "I'm not hungry." His eyes looked sad. But food was something too valuable to eat when you weren't hungry.

"Where do you fellows live?" I asked. Lindomar shrugged.

"Roberto and I share a box in the alley near the bank," said Newton. "Lindomar sleeps wherever he can find a spot."

"But don't you have a mother?"

Newton nodded. "She's never home," he said. "She works the streets. And when she is home, she's got a John and doesn't want me around."

I turned to Roberto. "What about you?"

"I'm not going home again."

"Why not?"

"Because he always beats me."

"Who?"

"My mother's man. He gets drunk and then he beats me."

"Why does he beat you?"

"I don't know. Because he's drunk, I guess. Or because I won't steal for him, or didn't get enough."

"Do you have brothers and sisters?"

"Ten," he said. "Sometimes I sneak back and see them in the afternoon. I'm the oldest. I have to kind of look out for them."

"How old are you?"

"Eleven," he said. Lindomar was happily tucking away the last bites of fish stew.

"What about you?" I said.

He smiled. "I've got no momma and papa," he said.

"How old are you?"

Again the shy smile. "I'm not sure," he said.

"He's seven," said Newton. "Or nine."

"I'm not sure," Lindomar said again.

"But I don't think I am older than Newton."

"Where are you going to sleep tonight?"

"Can I sleep at your house?" he said.

"My house is too far away. I'm sleeping on the boat."

"Can I sleep on the boat?"

"I don't know," I said. "I'm not sure how Sr. João will like it. But it's very dark down there along the quay. Maybe you can sneak on. But I can't promise they won't kick you back off."

Lindomar's bunny face broke into a big smile. "What's for dessert?" he said

By the time we had our cafezinhos, Newton and Lindomar had disappeared. Roberto was fast asleep in his chair. "Let him sleep," said Paulo when Julio came with the bill. "The kid isn't doing any harm."

Julio snorted. "True enough," he said. "At least when he is asleep he isn't stealing."

Paulo and I wandered back to the Moreira. There was a string of lights running from the pilot house back to the stern. I had forgotten about those. They would be turned out later, but only when Antonio returned to the boat sometime after midnight. Too late for Lindomar.

As usual, Sr. João was up, walking his son.

"Nice night," I said. "So clear."

"Pois é," he said, employing that universal Brazilian expression that means everything from "sure is" to "you're crazy," depending on your tone of voice.

The stars are fantastic," I said. "Pity you can't show them to Mrs. Moreira."

He looked at me.

"Why not?" he said.

"It's the boat," I said. "You can't see them from all that light."

Moreira grunted. "Good night," he said and walked off, bouncing his son.

The lights went out two minutes later. I don't know when Lindomar came aboard. Sometime in the night I woke and saw him huddled on the floor, next to the wall, out of the wind. We had no blankets and I went and put a shirt over him. He slept on without noticing. I went back to my hammock and I woke up again around 5:00 a.m. to the sounds of a thwack and a yelp.

"Out of here, you goddamn little thief!"

Enraba Onça had given Lindomar a sharp slap on the backside and he was now running off the gangplank and onto the quay.

"What did you do that for?" Paulo asked.

"Goddamn little thief," said Enraba Onça. "They're all little thieves."

"They're not, really," said Sr. Oswaldo, when I asked him later that morning.

"Oh, they may filch a bit, now and then. Wouldn't you? Now Newton, you've got to watch him. He's a little thief and a half. He'll have your money out of your pocket before you know it's gone. But Lindomar? I don't believe it..."

He paused and scratched his stomach. "I wonder how he came to be on board. He's never done that before..." Sr. Oswaldo gazed at me and popped another cracker into his mouth. "You're a nice fella," he said.

Before we turned in the car, Paulo wanted to find out for next year's trip, how the road was from Cuiaba, some 3,000 kilometers south and west, so we stopped at the bus station and garage.

It turned out that a maintenance truck had come in that morning from Cuiaba, and the driver, Barbosa, was still in the yard. We went out back to talk with him. Like most Brazilians,

Barbosa was an obliging fellow and he was only too happy to talk to us about the Cuiaba road.

"It was fine," he said. "Red earth all the way, and gas stations at least every 200 kilometers. Watch behind you."

I turned around. Just behind me on the concrete floor of the garage lay a piece of dirty fur which on closer inspection turned out to be a dead three-toed sloth (in Portuguese a "*preguiça*," or "laziness"). Only it wasn't dead. The poor beast lay spread-eagled on the floor a piece of yellow plastic rope around its middle, barely breathing.

"I picked it up off the road about 200 km out of Cochabamba," said Barbosa.

"It must have fallen out of a tree. I was going to take it back to Cuiaba for my little girl, but I don't think it will make it."

Paulo picked up one of the limp arms, then let it drop back to the floor. The three long, curved toenails looked entirely useless on the concrete.

"Why don't we put it on a tree?" he said.

Barbosa shrugged. "Why not?"

He picked up the plastic rope and we carried the beast across the yard to a cluster of Ipê trees growing next to the office. Barbosa set the sloth on the trunk of the largest tree. The arms and legs both reached around the tree, but the trunk was too big and it fell off.

"Try the smaller one," said Paulo.

Barbosa put the beast onto the next smaller tree and this

time the arms and legs held. Barbosa took off the rope, and slowly, ever so slowly, the sloth began to climb. In five minutes, it was up in the leaves, some 40 feet above the ground, and had disappeared.

Barbosa smiled. "Makes my day," he said.

"Bet we made his too," said Paulo. "Do you see a lot of animals along that road?"

"Sure do," said Barbosa.

"Even jaguars?"

"I must've seen 'em all."

"Well," said Barbosa, "The closest I ever came to a jaguar was a panther I didn't even see. A couple of years ago, the truck broke down about halfway from Cuiaba to Barra da Garça. It was getting late and I decided to walk to the next house for help. It turned out to be only six or seven kilometers away. As I approached the house, the farmer started shouting at me, pointing. I thought he was pointing at me. Then he ran into his house and came back out with a gun. I damn near died."

"There's a black panther," he shouted, "behind you."

"But when I turned it must have dashed for the wood. All I saw was the tail disappear into the brush. I don't know how long he had been following me as I walked along that road. But according to that farmer, he was no more than five meters behind me." Barbosa shrugged. "That's too close," he said.

We delivered the car back to the rental agency at the hotel and walked into town, looking behind us now and then. But there were only motorcycles and cars. Probably more dangerous than a panther, but less threatening. On the way in, we stopped along the quay and negotiated the rental of a boat to take us up some of the creeks off the main river, to Maringa. We chose the "Jorge Santos," a somewhat larger version of the African Queen, used by the owner, Sr. Santos, principally for moving freight - from bananas to tractors -anywhere along the river that anyone might want. And sometime he moved tourists.

The trip was unexciting, lots of marshes, herons and things, except for when I slipped and fell off the upper deck and damn near landed in a tributary that was full of piranhas. Since I had bounced off some equipment that was lashed to the lower deck, I was bleeding, too… I wasn't badly hurt, and we had a swim in the mighty Amazonas itself on the way back, after my wounds had dried.

Only a few minutes after we get back to the Moreira. Sr. Angelinho came aboard, carrying a mirror and a bag full of shaving gear, as well as another bag full of fishing tackle. We had seen Sr. Angelinho before, walking along the quay with his mirror, but hadn't known what it was for. Now he placed it carefully against one of the columns on the lower deck, arranged a stool from somewhere, took out his scissors, and began cutting Sr. Oswaldo's hair.

"Best barber in town," said Sr. Oswaldo.

"And the cheapest, too. You boys ought to get yours cut as well." Based on what was happening to Sr. Oswaldo's head, we decided against it, even if Sr. Angelinho was the best barber in all of Santarém. Oswaldo scowled.

"My wife prefers it long," I said.

He might not have had a talent for cutting hair, but what a fisherman! No sooner had Sr. Angelinho finished with Sr. Oswaldo's hair, he headed for the upper deck, pulled a line out of his fishing bag and sent it looping off the stern. Then he lit a cigarette, and looked down. With his other hand, he held the line up over his head.

"Well," he said into the water, "come on, I haven't got all night."

The first giant catfish hit the line less than a minute later. I saw Sr. Angelinho give a giant leap backward, arm still in the air, and then begin rapidly hauling in the line, hand over hand.

"Got him," he said. "20 kilos to the gram."

The Amazon catfish, or Piraiba, is an ugly fish, a flabby, fat matron with a large grey mustache. And enormous. Sr. Angelinho maneuvered the fish around to the side of the boat, then slowly raised it up, until it cleared the rail of the lower deck. Then, giving the line a jerk from above, he sent the beast flying over the rail and onto the lower deck.

"My God. He'll be eating fish for a week," said Paulo.

But in the next half hour, seven more giant catfish came flying onto the lower deck. After the first two, Sr. Angelinho got out a few more lines and passed them around, and before long everyone was catching fish. Paulo caught one, I caught one but it got away, Antonio caught one, Tania caught an enormous one, but couldn't pull it up to the lower deck, so Antonio had to help. By the time the night turned black and the swallows were settled in, there were eight huge, ugly dead fish on the lower deck.

"Does he keep them all?" I asked Antonio.

"Of course," he said. "They were his lines, weren't they?"

Sr. Angelinho was still putting away his lines when I came back upstairs.

"What do you do with all that fish?" I asked. "You must sell it."

He looked surprised.

"Sell it? No. Who'd buy it?" he said. "I salt it, and we dry it in the sun, just like the sun dried meat, our *carne de sol*. It lasts forever that way. When you want to eat it, you just soak it in some good river water, Throw away the water, then cook it any way you like. That's what the Portuguese do with cod, you know. Only Piraiba is more delicious. You gringos might not like it, of course, but you don't know what's good." He grinned.

Dinner that night was back at Julio's. We invited Tania, and after some hesitation, she came. None of us wanted fish, or sun dried meat either, and we were glad that Julio had cooked up a *feijoada*, a thick black bean stew with sausage and pig's ears and just a little sun dried meat for flavor, Julio said. The *feijoada* was delicious, washed down with icy cold beer. We talked about Sr. Angelinho and the fishing, and it wasn't until we were almost finished that we noticed that Newton wasn't there.

Roberto and Lindomar stood in the shadows, beyond the

light from the restaurant. Without Newton, they seemed afraid to come over. We motioned for them to come.

"Where is Newton?" I asked. Roberto looked solemn, as always.

"He went to Manaus," he said.

"But that's a huge city," said Paulo, "and it's far away. Does he know someone there?"

Roberto shrugged. "I don't think so," he said.

"But how will he get there?"

"He stowed away on the Paulo Melo Franco," he said. "You can't catch him anymore. She left at 2:30 today."

"How do you know?"

"Because Lindomar told me."

I turned to Lindomar. He still looked like a pet bunny, but I think he was a little mad at me. Somehow, Enraba Onça's swat was considered to be my fault. "Did you see him leave?"

"No, I haven't seen him since the Melo Franco left." said Lindomar. "But he told me he was going."

We were horrified. How would a nine year old survive in Manaus, with no money, or family or friends.

"What happens if they find him on the boat?" I asked.

Julio had come over to clear the table. "They'll slap him in a kids home, that's what. Ought to throw him in jail if you ask me." He picked up the bowl of *feijoada*, still half full of black beans and black-cooked meat. Lindomar watched in silence.

"Wait," said Tania. "I think I'll eat a little more of that."

She looked at Lindomar, then at Roberto. "Do you think you fellows could help?"

Julio scowled a phony scowl. "There was some rice got sent back by another table," he said. "I guess you might as well eat that, too." He headed off to get it.

"Bring some cold beers," said Paulo. "And a glass for yourself."

"Like I said before, you're a sensible fellow," Julio said.

Lindomar and Roberto finished off the rice and the *feijoada* and disappeared, and the four of us continued drinking frosty Brahma Chopp and talking until the Amazon moon had passed overhead and was moving west.

"Closing time," said Julio at last. "Even in Santarém, tomorrow is another day."

"And our last," said Paulo.

"Can't be," I said. "It's only been a couple of days."

Tania smiled at me. "Paulo's right," she said.

"The Moreira leaves tomorrow at 5:00 p.m. for Manaus. Let's head back to the boat."

The moonlight came in through the porthole of Tania's tiny cabin. My mind was on a little boy hiding somewhere on another steamer, heading up the great river to Manaus.

"Do you think he'll be all right?" I asked her.

Tania smiled a sleepy smile, and ran her fingers down my chest. "You're a nice man," she said, and then she fell asleep.

The Moreira da Silva III left Santarém the next evening

amidst great clanging of bells and general uproar, at 7:00 p.m., only two hours late.

"Incredible," said Paulo, as we watched her pulling away from the quay.

"Truly," I said. We were both quite drunk.

About 4:00 p.m. Enraba Onça had come back aboard with a large green glass jug of cachaça, which Antonio, Paulo and I helped him finish. By 4:45, we had given great abraços to Sr. Oswaldo, Sr. João, Antonio (several times), Sr. Gato, Tania and just about all of the crew, and had gone ashore to watch her leave. At five minutes to five, a yellow pickup came careening down the quay, carrying what looked like a huge marine engine. The damn thing must have weighed several tons, even Antonio was unable to budge it without help. With a lot of grunting and groaning, the boys managed to get it off the truck and onto the quay, but there it sat. It would go no further. Sr. Gato tried lashing some heavy ropes around it, with the idea of swinging it onto the lower deck like a catfish, but Sr. Oswaldo persuaded him that the damn thing was likely to go right through the side of the boat. More ropes, more consultations, at least twenty self-styled experts giving expert advice from shore. Someone thought to call Sr. Moreira but he was in his cabin and declined to come out.

It was Paulo who finally solved the problem.

"How about the boards that Sr. Moreira's car came aboard on?" he said. "We'll grease it up with some of Antonio's engine grease." Everyone stopped talking, and Antonio went below and brought up the grease and the boards.

"What if they don't hold?" someone asked.

Antonio grinned. "It'll be a water cooled engine," he said. They held.

In less than 15 minutes, the boys had greased up the boards and slid the engine onto the lower deck, just below where Sr. Angelinho had been fishing the night before. Then they lashed it down. Sr. Gato walked back to the bridge and started clanging bells, Antonio disappeared into the engine room, a few hangers-on leaped for the shore and the Moreira da Silva III slid out from the quay, turned in the muddy water and started to move slowly upstream. Sr. João appeared at the rail holding his son.

"Come join us again," he called above the engines.

Paulo gave a thumbs-up sign. "We'll be back."

"Com certeza, for sure" he shouted.

We walked back into town for a final dinner at Julio's. Newton was sitting there waiting for us when we arrived. We stopped dead in our tracks.

"Too much cachaça," said Paulo, rubbing his eyes. But Newton was real.

"I thought you went to Manaus," I said.

"I changed my mind."

"But where were you last night?"

"At home. Mom didn't have any Johns, so I thought I'd go back." He smiled a wonderful shy smile. "Be dumb to travel when the eating's good here. It's not every day we get a big-eating gringo in Santarém."

That night we bought him his own sirloin steak. But before he ate it, he went and found Roberto and Lindomar so they could share. Julio damn near died. We slept in the Santarém Centro Palace Hotel, just next to Ronaldo's house on the bank of the river. The hotel was, of course, a dump, but it had hammock hooks. We missed the motion of the river, but our hammocks were far better than the beds. We slept well.

At about 6:00 a.m. I awoke. From just outside the window someone was shouting "eh" which in Portuguese means "it is". I opened the shutter, and there, in a huge purple Ipê tree almost directly outside the window sat a great red macaw, shouting "eh" at the dawn. Paulo jumped out of his hammock and to the window.

"Is this a great place?" he shouted.

"Eh," said the bird.

"Is the Moreira a great boat?"

"Eh," said the bird.

"Is Ronaldo a son of a bitch?"

"Eh," said the bird.

Just then, a sliver of sun rose over the river.

Paulo grinned. "Guess it's time to go," he said.

"Eh," said the bird.

THE BLACK OLDSMOBILE

To begin, as they say, at the beginning: I grew up in a little jerkwater town on eastern Long Island called Center Moriches. Its main distinction was that it was located next to East Moriches, a little town which called itself the "Duck Capital of the World". That was because East Moriches claimed the largest number of duck farms and the largest population of edible ducks per capita of any place in the world. This did not require all that many ducks since there were only about 300 human "capita" who lived in East Moriches. The ducks defecated in the salt water creeks which emptied into Moriches Bay.

All this is really beside the point of my story, but it does give you an idea of what Center Moriches was all about. Center had a population of about 2,000. Perhaps 50 families were African American. There wasn't a lot of reason to move there except that, since the odor of duck filth often wafted from the duck farms in East Moriches, property tax was a good deal lower than in other towns nearby. That was a major factor for my father, who spent his life believing that some authority or other would declare him to be bankrupt by sometime next week. Cheaper was better. My father bought our house on Beachfern Road in Center Moriches in September 1945 for five thousand dollars. I was 11 years old. My mother took me to the public school up on the hill the day after we moved in. They put me in the 5th grade. There was one thing that struck me as different when I arrived for my first day of school. Clustered in the back of the classroom were 7 or 8 black kids, most of them a good deal bigger than me. In Glen Ridge, New Jersey, where we lived before moving to Long Island, there had been no black kids in my class nor even, as far as I knew, in the whole school. Center Moriches was different. So what? So one helluva lot! And that's what my story is all about.

So suppose you were an African American kid in the fifth grade in the Center Moriches Elementary School. You probably lived in the rough neighborhood across the tracks. You might be 10, but you also might be 12 or 13. Then one day, this nerdy little white kid shows up in class, a little pudgy and wearing thick oversized glasses who correctly answers every question the teacher asks. He is annoying. So what do you do? You beat the hell out of him, that's what you do.

In those days the black and white sections of town were totally separate, totally alien worlds. Most of the other white kids lived a distance from the school and rode the bus home. I lived close enough to walk, so after school there was just me, a bunch of the African Americans and one big white kid.

They were waiting outside the back door when I walked out my first day. At first they just stood there looking at me. Then, suddenly, a scrawny little black girl threw herself at me while her brother stuck a foot between my legs from behind. I went down onto the concrete with her on top of me, beating my face with her fists. Nerdy little fool that I was, I didn't think I could fight back because she was a girl and you didn't fight girls. But pretty soon I was sorry I didn't. She grabbed my left ear lobe with her teeth and bit down hard. The blood trickled onto my white shirt while her brother and a couple of other boys gave me a couple of well-placed kicks in the ribs. It was about then that I learned what the big white kid was there for, he was the referee.

"Alright Janice, you, too, Sylvester," he said to the girl and her brother, "that's enough." Sylvester took one last kick at me. "You'd better go home now," the big white kid said to me. "Better run."

I didn't need for him to tell me twice. Although my back was badly scratched and my ribs were pretty sore, the only thing my mother noticed when I got home was my ear.

"What happened?" she asked.

"I fell off my bike," I said. "The chain got my ear."

I knew she didn't believe me, but she didn't say anything more. I slept that night on the right side of my head, with my injured left ear in the air. I was so nervous the next morning I could hardly eat breakfast. I left for school hoping yesterday's beating was a onetime thing, "welcome to Center Moriches" so to speak. But I wasn't that lucky.

When last class bell rang, I ducked out the front door rather than the back. It didn't work. They must have had a scout. In a few seconds, the mob charged around the corner of the building. A black kid named George who I hadn't seen the day before and who was even bigger than the rest, grabbed me by the shoulder and punched me in the stomach. My glasses flew off.

"Come on," he said "Fight."

Another kid stepped forward and punched me in the eye, just as the front door of the school opened, and the principal, Mr. Privett, strode out.

"Leave him alone, you bunch of chickens," he bellowed. "All you guys against one little white kid. You're a lily livered bunch of turds."

He turned to me. "You'd better head home. And take care of that black eye."

The next day, the rules changed. I had expected that things might even get worse, but when the final bell rang, Mrs. Meier, the home room teacher, scowled at the whole group of black kids who were moving toward the door.

"Back in your seats," she snapped, "and open your notebooks. You're staying 10 more minutes. And Peter, you go right home." That was Wednesday. The same thing happened

Thursday and Friday. That was swell but those rules couldn't go on forever, and those kids were just going to get madder and madder as the days went on. Besides, it didn't seem fair to the kids who hadn't participated in the beatings, but who were held after school as well.

I finally told my mother what was going on. "Don't tell me," she said, "tell Mrs. Meier. Tell her the part about it not being fair, but make sure you do it when the other kids can hear you. Then tell her you want her to let them all leave when you do."

So Monday afternoon, when Sylvester, Janice and Big George were standing around near Mrs. Meier's desk, I asked her to let them all go when I left that afternoon. She looked at me. "Are you sure? Does your mom agree?" she asked. "If that's your choice, I guess you're entitled to it."

My tormentors were all there that afternoon when I walked out the back door. Nobody said anything. Nobody moved, except Janice who moved close to me, curling her hand into a fist. It was very quiet. One kid reached out and grasped her hand.

"No," he said. "That's enough." I learned his name was Bobby Burwell.

I had no more trouble with them the rest of the year. They didn't bother me, but they weren't exactly my friends either. They just acted as though I didn't exist, which was alright for me. That spring, about a month before final exams, Mrs. Meier asked me to stay after school one afternoon.

"You know Bobby Burwell?" she asked. Of course I knew

Bobby. He was the kid who had stopped Janice from continuing the beating 6 months ago.

"Well," Mrs. Meier went on, "he's not going to graduate to sixth grade." Now, for some strange reason, the business people in Center Moriches considered graduation into 6th grade particularly important. If you graduated into 6th grade, you had a much better chance of getting some kind of job. If not, you had no chance at all.

"How come he won't graduate?"

"Math," Mrs. Meier continued. "He's fine with everything else, but he just doesn't get mathematics. Would you be willing to try to tutor him?"

That afternoon when the closing bell rang, I headed over to his desk before he could get up.

"Bobby," I said, "I hear you're having some trouble with math. Maybe I could help out."

"Get the hell out of here," he said. He got up and started toward the door. "You don't owe me nuthin," he said. "Not a damn thing. You got that?" Then he was gone.

But the next afternoon, just as I was leaving the room, I heard Bobby say, "Wait a minute, asshole." We both waited until everyone else had left the room.

"I ain't talked a word to you. And you ain't talked a word to me. You got that?"

"Okay," I said, "I promise."

"Alright," Bobby said, "now tell me what these goddamn

numbers are all about."

Bobby passed the math final, but I had nothing to do with it. Well, in a way I did. The day before the final exam, I ran into Mr. Privett in the hall. "Mrs. Meier tells me you're helping Bobby Burwell with his math. How's he doing?"

"He won't pass the final, Mr. Privett" I said. "He just doesn't get math. There's nothing more I can do."

The principal looked very serious. "Maybe there is," he said. "Maybe there is."

The test the next day was easier than I had imagined and I was finished and on my way out in less than half an hour. Bobby was sitting at his desk across the aisle from mine. He hadn't finished the first question on the test. It was about then that Mrs. Meier walked out of the room and Mr. Privett walked in. Mrs. Meier was indisposed, he said, and was going home. I picked up my exam to bring it up to Mr. Privett.

"That's alright, Peter," he said. "You can just leave it on your desk." I got an A on the test. Bobby got a C+.

Mr. Privett and I got to be great friends over the years. And one day I finally asked him, "There's one thing I've always wanted to know, Mr. Privett. How did Bobby Burwell get a C+ on that math exam 10 years ago?" The principal's eyes smiled.

"You did that," he said. "You wrote your exam clearly enough that anyone could copy it."

"Yes, but I didn't let him copy my exam. You're the only one who could have given it to him. But, you're the principal, for

Christ sakes."

"Look," Privett said. "If I hadn't done anything, Bobby was going to flunk out and ruin his chances of getting an honest job. But if I just closed my eyes for a few minutes, I could give Bobby a chance in life, without it costing anyone. Lots of people close their eyes to the wrong things. This was the right thing."

Bobby did flunk out in the seventh grade but not before he got a job as a mechanic at Ziadnitski's garage. I also did a little tutoring for the Wimball brothers, John and Rosko. They made it into 8ᵗʰ grade. So did Sylvester Q, but without my help. Janice got pregnant at 16 and had triplets.

*****

By the time they were fifteen, quite a few of the African American kids in town had their own cars: Buicks, Caddies, Oldsmobiles. I have no idea how they could afford them. All of them were huge, spotlessly clean, and beautifully polished. They burned eight or nine miles a gallon, but that didn't matter much in those days, since gas cost only about 20 cents a gallon for high test. They all smelled of sweet fake pine from the little cardboard trees which dangled from their rear view mirrors.

I was the only white kid in the town who knew what the insides of those cars smelled like. That was because I was the only white kid who ever rode in one of those cars, and I did so fairly often. My first ride happened one Saturday evening in my sophomore year of high school when the chain popped off my bike on Montauk Highway. I was struggling unsuccessfully to get it back on when a shiny black and silver Oldsmobile pulled up and stopped next to me. It was Big George who by then was 16, and had gotten himself a seriously nasty reputation. The word around town was that he had, earlier in the year, cut the ear off a kid from Mattituck who had failed to show George appropriate respect. I wasn't terribly glad to see him.

"Hey Pete," George said. "Watsa' matter? Chain popped off? Broke, huh?" I felt a little better. George wouldn't want the bike if it was broken. "Put it in the trunk and get in," George said. He opened the trunk. I squeezed the bike in and started to crawl in on top of it as he had instructed. George smiled for the first time.

"Not you, you idiot. You put the bike in the trunk. You get in the front seat."

George drove me down Main Street, and home. The people on Main Street who saw me in George's car gaped. Later, they told me they simply couldn't believe it. Not a white kid, not in George's car.

I guess the word got around the community north of the tracks that if George could give me a ride, they could too. White people in Center Moriches weren't all that likely to pick you up if you were hitchhiking home from work or caught in the rain. But in my last two years of high school, I never stood by the side of the road waiting for a ride for more than five minutes. Every one of the guys who picked me up was black. And every one drove me all the way to my house and down the driveway, in the white part of town. Riding down Main Street in one of those big, shiny cars were my proudest moments at Center Moriches High School. No other white kid got to do that.

There was one time, though, that George gave me a ride that scared me half to death. I worked, at the time, as a dishwasher at the Sunrise Restaurant. It was Friday night, and I had just been paid. I wandered down Main Street to Vinnie Drevas' soda fountain. I sat down at the counter and ordered a cup of coffee and a piece of pie. In one of the booths at the back, I noticed George and a guy I didn't know who was even bigger than George and just as tough looking. I was sipping my second cup of coffee when I asked Vinnie for the check. In my wallet were a $20 and a single, my salary for the week. I pulled out the single. The $20 bill stuck to it, slid out of my wallet, and fluttered slowly to the ground. I dove to the floor to pick it up, but everyone had seen it.

George got up and walked slowly to the counter. "Get in the car," he snarled.

"George, I haven't finished my coffee." George's hand slammed down, and moved fast across the counter. The coffee cup went flying, sending coffee in every direction before the cup shattered on the tile floor. George's voice dropped an octave. It was terrifying now.

"You've finished your damn coffee. Now get in the car." I walked out Vinnie's door, over to George's car and got in.

"Where are we going George?"

"Shut up," he said.

George burned rubber leaving the soda fountain, spun down to the third corner heading for East Moriches, burned some more rubber turning onto Beachfern Road, then into our driveway.

"You are the stupidest asshole I've ever met," he said. I decided it was smarter to say nothing. "You know who that guy with me at Vinnie's was?"

I shook my head.

"That's Eddie Willard out of Brooklyn. They're looking for him for murder. He killed a guy in a holdup on Flatbush Avenue. And you wave a fucking $20 bill under his nose. Now take your goddamn money into the house, and don't come back out until Monday."

I got out of the car. "Thanks George," I said.

He glared at me, slammed his car into reverse, and burned rubber again as he backed his Oldsmobile out the driveway.

But it wasn't until I was in college that George and his friends finally and definitively made up for the welcome they gave me in the 5th grade, even though they didn't even know they were doing it.

At Christmas I generally came home early from college and had a job selling shoes in the evenings in Riverhead, the county seat. One night about 10 p.m. I left the shop and was walking to my car when I noticed them. This was Riverhead. I didn't know the guys a block behind me, following me in the dark. I tried walking faster, they kept up. There was a street light half a block ahead of me. I sped up and stopped when I reached it. They caught up.

"Hey buddy," the youngest one said, "you got a light?"

Original line, I thought. "Sure," I said. "But you guys know Bobby Burwell over in Center Moriches?"

The kid looked a little puzzled. "Yeah," he said.

"How about John and Rosko Wimball?" They started to look a little nervous.

"Yeah, we know 'em."

"Sylvester and Janice Q?" I asked. They nodded. I decided to play my ace. "You know George Rowland? The really big guy, who drives a black Olds?"

There was terror in their eyes now. "Yeah man, we know George."

"Well," I said, "they're all good friends of mine... now do you still want that light?"

"No, man," he said, "We don't need no light."

The three of them turned and walked quickly away into the night. I told George about it when I saw him in Center Moriches a week later. It was the only time I ever saw George laugh. "Little pricks," he said.

The public schools in Center Moriches were no great academic shakes. I didn't learn much mathematics there either. But you could, if you wanted, learn something about life and how to get through the rest of it.

Thank you Mr. Privett. Thank you Big George.

1939

The young man leaned back against the rusted iron cross that marked the summit.

"Damn, it's cold," he said.

Below, in the moonlight, he could see their tracks on the Swiss side of the border where they curved through the snow around an outcropping of granite and then curved back up again through the white snow until they disappeared in the shadows behind the granite and the snow. With his field glasses, he could make out where they had left their skis and their packs and continued on snowshoes to the summit. Two red flags marked the border. A white cross on one and a black swastika on the other.

"Happy Easter," the guide said. He was rolling a cigarette with his gloves on.

"Frohe Ostern," the younger man said. "You have been a

guide on the Wildspitze often? I mean at Easter?"

"Yes. But only from Austria to Switzerland since the Anschluss annexation. Not the other way. We could still go back, you know."

"No," the young man said. Far to the South he could see Monte Rosa slowly turning pink.

"We'd better go," the guide said. "You'll need your goggles." They walked back down to where the skis were planted in the snow. They were wood, painted white, with sealskins strapped to the bottom. "You won't need the skins," the guide said.

He was a good skier, and it was not hard to follow the tracks that were left by the guide. The snow was dry and the sun came up cold behind him, and he skied fast behind his shadow on the snow. Later he passed a tree. They had been above timberline for three days, and it was good to see a tree.

He crouched into a schuss position to catch the guide, but he was far down, and now there were more trees. They were spruce and he could smell the sap rising.

Further down, he caught up. "The snow will be wetter now," the guide said. He paused a moment. "Can I ask you a question?"

"Sure."

"Your name is not Wilson, it is Weinfeld. David Weinfeld."

"Yes. How did you know?"

The guide didn't answer.

"Yes."

"You are Jewish," he said. "Why are you going to Austria?"

"Because my wife is there. She is waiting at the Hotel Weisser Hirsch in Hochsolden. We will go back to Switzerland the same way we came."

"That is very dangerous. You must love her very much."

"Yes. Very much."

They skied on, and the snow turned to slush, and now he could smell the earth and the manure in the valley. The snow grew patchy, and finally it was gone and they were in a pasture with mud everywhere. It smelled of springtime. They took off their skis, and walked through the mud with their skis on their shoulders and the mud on their boots.

"You will take us back?" the young man asked.

The guide looked tired. "Yes," he said. "It is harder, leaving Austria...It is very dangerous," he said again.

"Thank you" the young man said softly.

He walked on through the mud toward the town.

THE SHIRT

I came across the shirt again the other day, in the back of my summer closet. It's a wreck, roughly 60 years old by now, and showing every day of it. I haven't worn it for 50 years. The outside is a sort of dirty grey with what used to be a few narrow cross-hatched stripes. On the inside, you can tell they were once blue and green and red. The material is heavy cotton that looks like an irate tiger has tried to tear it to shreds, God knows why. There are ragged holes everywhere, one of the pockets has been completely torn off.

Sewn inside on what's left of the collar is a "name tag" reading "PETER HORNBOSTEL". Summer camp required those.

I have tried to throw out that shirt at least a dozen times, but I never succeed. About 20 or 30 years ago, when it still fit me, more or less, I thought I might still use it for gardening, but I don't garden. Then, when it started to become really ratty, I would periodically decide to throw it out, and then "forget" and hang it back in the rear of the closet. When I moved to Brazil in the 90s, I was sure I had thrown it out, only to discover it in the attic in a box of old clothes when I returned. A year ago, it actually made it in its journey to the trash can outside the house.

The day the garbage truck was scheduled to come by, I woke up early, dashed outside in my pajamas, and fished it out of the trash can a few minutes before the truck came down the street. That shirt and I go back a long way, back to when I was 11, or maybe 12.

I was one of those kids who got sent away to summer camp every year, so their parents could have some time by themselves. I think my mother felt just a little guilty about that. Anyway, she bought me this shirt as a sort of a consolation prize for not going with them to Maine. She got it a few sizes too big so it would last a few years. I wore it everywhere. Like I told you, the shirt was cotton, and it wasn't really warm. But I wore it anyway over just a tee shirt, even in the cool August evenings in upstate New York. It was warm enough.

I didn't know anything about love back then, but there was a girl at camp maybe a year or two older than I, who left me breathless every time I saw her. I can't really remember for sure whether she was beautiful, but I like to think she was. She was a tomboy, with dirty blonde hair and a suntan and freckles, just like a tomboy was supposed to have. Far ahead of her time, she wore jeans which were just tight enough to get her in trouble with the head counselor. I think she had a wonderful little pushed up nose, but that could be my imagination. Her name was "Vergine," but everybody called her Ginny.

Ginny never spoke to me until the night of the campfire, nor, as far as I could tell, ever looked at me either. Every week or so, unless it was too cold, there was a campfire after dark. Murray Phillips, the swim counselor, played his guitar and sang songs like the ones The Mammas and the Pappas made popular many years later. A few of the older boys, 14 and 15, sat on blankets with their girlfriends under the watchful eyes of the counselors.

It was the last campfire of the year, and I was sitting on the other side of the fire, freezing in my shirt. Murray was singing "Roll on, Columbia, roll on", when I saw Ginny crawling up to the fire, not 15 feet away from me. My heart stopped. She paused, and sat on the ground - no blanket - for a minute or maybe two. Then, still on her hands and knees, she came crawling over to my blanket. She brought her head over to my left ear (I've kept that, too) and whispered, "I'm cold." I thought I was going to die.

"Here," I gasped. "Take my shirt." She put it on and gave me a sort of funny look. Then she leaned her gorgeous body against me. As I remember, I did nothing at all...except die. Like I said, what did I know about love back then?

The last week of camp that year was one of the happiest weeks of my life. Ginny held onto the shirt, and every time I saw her in it, my heart gave a little jump. She wore it all the time. We went everywhere together, walks, the waterfront, the craft house. The camp director, God bless him, even put us at the same table in the dining hall. Of course, I never touched her, other than to hold her hand whenever we walked anywhere together, she in my shirt, and me walking on air.

Suddenly it was over. The camp hired two buses to take us to the train to go to New York to Cooperstown, and home. Ginny sat with her girlfriends at the other end of the car laughing and shrieking and hollering and paying me no attention. She wasn't wearing my shirt. I walked past them at least three times, supposedly on my way to the toilet, but she ignored me.

I was pretty miserable by the time we reached Grand Central and everyone tumbled off the train and said their goodbyes. I stood there in the station looking around for my mother, when suddenly Ginny was standing in front of me. "That was really fun," she said. And then she kissed me on the lips. I'm surprised I ever washed my mouth again.

I only saw Ginny again once after that. The camp had a reunion in New York every year, I usually didn't go. But that year was different. I had written some 15 letters to Ginny since the summer ended, but hadn't mailed one of them. And I hadn't gotten a letter from Ginny either. But if we saw each other at the reunion, we could talk and be together. Maybe she would even wear my shirt. Or kiss me again. I signed up to attend.

Still, I heard nothing from Ginny.

And then, a few days before the reunion, I received an

envelope postmarked "Larchmont, N.Y." It was from Ginny.

"Peter," it read.

"Are you going to the reunion? If so, my mother says you can have lunch here first. Vergine."

I was overjoyed.

I arrived at Ginny's house the day of the reunion. What happened then, has happened to me once or twice again, later in life. Ginny opened the door and stood there in a pink organdy dress and white pumps. Her hair was clean and blonde. I think she even wore lipstick, but I'm not sure.

Ginny extended her hand to me. ""Hello Peter. Won't you come in?"

It was gone. The magic was gone.

Somehow we made it through lunch. Fortunately, Ginny's mother chattered nonstop. "Did I like school? Did I do sports? Had I liked camp? How about the spinach?" Ginny said almost nothing.

After lunch, I made an excuse having to stop back early at my mother's house on Long Island before the reunion began. Ginny saw me to the door. Again she extended her hand.

"Goodbye, Peter," she said. I was almost out the door when she stopped me.

"Oh, I almost forgot," she said. She ran back into the house and came back with a brown paper bag. "This is yours, I think," she said.

I took the bag and turned to go.

"You know, it really was fun," she said, just before she shut the door.

Made in the USA
Columbia, SC
02 December 2020

26096765R00102